CADILLAC COUCHES

Cadillac Couches

Sophie B. Watson

BRINDLE
& GLASS

Brindle & Glass Publishing Ltd.
brindleandglass.com

LIBRARY AND ARCHIVES CANADA CATALOGUING IN PUBLICATION
Watson, Sophie B., 1972–
Cadillac couches / Sophie B. Watson.

Issued also in electronic formats.
ISBN 978-1-926972-90-9

I. Title.

PS8645.A873C34 2012   C813'.6   C2012-902557-7

Editor: Lynne Van Luven
Copy Editor/Proofreader: Heather Sangster, Strong Finish
Design and cover illustration: Pete Kohut
Author photo: Aengus Kelly

Brindle & Glass is pleased to acknowledge the financial support for its publishing
program from the Government of Canada through the Canada Book Fund, Canada
Council for the Arts, and the Province of British Columbia through the British
Columbia Arts Council and the Book Publishing Tax Credit.

MIX
Paper from
responsible sources
FSC
www.fsc.org   FSC® C016245

The interior pages of this book have been printed on 100% post-consumer
recycled paper, processed chlorine free, and printed with vegetable-based inks.

This book is a work of fiction. Some of the characters in this story are based on real
people (namely Ani DiFranco, Dan Bern, and Hawksley Workman), but their
dialogue and actions are fictionalized. I have also taken liberties with the chronology
of their careers and songs. Other artists' songs time travel here and there throughout the
story. Other characters are purely products of my imagination, although they get
up to shenanigans in many of my favourite real places in Edmonton and across
Canada. Otherwise, any resemblances to actual people are entirely coincidental.

1 2 3 4 5 16 15 14 13 12

PRINTED IN CANADA

For Françoise and Garfield
with gratitude

and

To the memory of two super-Edmontonian
loved ones *and great music fanatics!*

Vanessa Hughes (1968–2009)
Lorne Johanson (1964–2011)

"When I tell you that I love you
Don't test my love
Accept my love, don't test my love
Cause maybe I don't love you all that much . . ."
"Jerusalem," Dan Bern

Bern Baby Bern

I let them help me up. The security people and accident group-ies dispersed. People probably assumed I had eaten too many magic mushrooms, a common festival mistake. Finn gave me some ginger ale to sip. I guzzled it back and Isobel gave me some comforting pretzels to munch on.

I was a goof—who fainted at gigs? It wasn't like we'd been watching Elvis performing "Suspicious Minds" in his full leathers and gyrating himself into a frenzy (now *that* would be enough reason to faint). How was I gonna cope when we met Dan Bern later?

Finn looked a bit weirded out. He had those cartoon eyes that bulged during normal times—possibly a thyroid thing—and in heightened times, they looked like two big sunny-side-up eggs with black olives for pupils.

"I saw the whole thing. You were staring at the stage, smil-ing. I mean, beaming like someone who's touched and about to speak in tongues. And then the longer he dragged out that 'mes-siahhhhhh' note in 'Jerusalem,' you looked like you were going to scream, or cry. You got quite red in the face and just, just as the cymbals started clashing at the end of the drummer's solo, you went down hard, but with a smile on your face. Boom!"

Finn demonstrated with his hands the kind of splatting effect my body had on the ground. "I mean, I can understand the excitement. They were rocking all right, but I'm not that sure it's healthy to pass out at gigs. That's twice now. You sure you're not allergic to something, like patchouli . . . ?"

"No, it's totally ridiculous . . . I know . . . I know. I'm some kind of train wreck."

One word lodged itself in my brain: *defeated.* And so I rushed toward it, open-armed. Hugging it.

Defeated.

So Defeated. Could be a chorus.

"Ma chérie, you're très sensitive. Think of Teresa in *The Unbearable Lightness of Being,*" Isobel said, inhabiting one of her bilingual moods. It always got on my nerves that she got to be the self-possessed Sabine character and I was always cast as the insecure Tereza.

"You're not a weirdo, me ducky," Finn soothed. "We've all got our strange stuff. I get so nervous on escalators, I almost always feel like throwing up in random women's purses. It's like that writer says, you know who I'm talking about, whatshername, anyways: life screws up *everyone* in some way. You just need a nice cup of tea."

I should've brought my smelling salts with me—bath salts worked well enough. When I got the woozy feeling, I just needed a snort of something strong, like Ocean Mist, to bring me back to my senses. Ironically, my dream had come true: I was at last living in a Victorian novel, but I wasn't a burgundy-velvet-cloaked heroine with long curly locks, roaming the Yorkshire moors on a black horse. I was one of those swooning characters, a histrionic whinger like those Jane Austen invented as a warning to flaky women throughout the ages. I didn't want to be confined to bed, even if it was a canopy one with billowing sheets and elaborate linens. Surely I was destined for a more rollicking ride of a life. I rallied my spirits by thinking of Hawksley's words of wisdom: "Don't act broken, even when you're broken . . ."

Despite everyone's better judgment, including my own, I went to get myself a Big Rock Grasshöpper wheat ale and had another cigarette to revive myself. I sucked on it indignantly, puffing out angry clouds of Benson & Hedges white smoke. But taking super-extended drags like that finished the cigarette off too fast. I needed more nicotine right away but didn't dare light up again with Isobel and Finn staring me down.

Isobel insisted on walking me around the grounds for a few laps to make sure I was steady. She let me bring my beer, expertly pouring it into her antique silver flask. She stashed the flask in the alligator green, vintage Prada purse that she was never without. Her favourite aunt had given it to her on her twenty-first birthday. Despite our differences, mainly her being into haute couture and me into hippie grunge, she was how I imagined a sister to be. Iz and I had been best friends since we were fifteen—nine long years of capers and larks.

We met each other for the first time at our most cherished place in town, the Princess Theatre on Whyte Avenue (it was our *Cinema Paradiso*). The red velvet curtains and lush, old-style red velvet upholstered seats were more like armchairs than theatre seats. The whole place pulsed with a vaudevillian red glow and smelled of magic: salty butter and stale smoke mixed with a dash of Chaplin-era mould. It was a Saturday matinee in autumn. We were the only two people there and I recognized her from my school. We had never talked before.

The Princess was a cultural gateway—it gave us the world beyond our mind-numbingly boring urban prairie; it gave us European cinema. Brooding men, smoking women, grand tours, sad endings, great styles, shocking discoveries, unbearable romance, lewd sex—real life! *Betty Blue, The Unbearable Lightness of Being, Diva, La Femme Nikita, The Big Blue,* Merchant and Ivory. When our schoolmates were smacking pucks around the local hockey arena or sipping hot chocolate at the world's biggest mall, we were busy trying to emulate Emmanuelle Béart's pout in *Manon des Sources.*

That Saturday the strange girl and I were both there to see *A Room with a View*, again. Walking in, I felt awkward, like when you're only one of two people on a bus, do you sit near or far apart? I felt it would be even more awkward not to acknowledge her, so I introduced myself. She suggested we pool resources: I had popcorn and she had M&Ms. We both had braces on our teeth and great expectations.

She'd seen the film six times and I'd seen it five during its two-week run at the Princess. Since then, over the years we've probably watched it together hundreds of times. Once we met Finn, we made him watch *A Room* too. He confessed that John Hughes's *Pretty in Pink, The Breakfast Club*, and *Ferris Bueller's Day Off* had dominated his romantic psyche until we introduced him to the thrill of George and Lucy's turn-of-the-century highbrow tennis romance. He loved the idea of us being these foul-mouthed Albertan-wannabe-Edwardians drinking Pimm's whenever we could. We studied the characters' every moves, both of us desperately wanting to be Lucy Honeychurch, all three of us swooning over the pair's kiss under the baking sun in the poppy fields overlooking Florence—what could be better? We vowed we'd make it to Florence one day.

Finn was a new Edmontonian, all the way from the Maritimes via Toronto for a few years. He had the true Maritimer spirit, all warmth, Celtic strangeness, and gregariousness; he played guitar not fiddle. Over the past year we had become friends at Rigoletto's restaurant where he and I worked, serving up gnocchi and Grappa to downtowners. Isobel had never dated someone from the Eastern Seaboard before and hadn't been able to resist sampling him. He didn't realize he was only an amuse bouche on her menu of men. She had an anthropologist's approach to dating, with categories ranging from geographic, cultural, aesthetic, to occupational. She was proudest of having dated a postcard publisher—very few people had the inside scoop on that scene.

Meanwhile, I had declared myself out of the dating/mating game for a few months. I was in a reinvention period and on a dating diet. On my new romance-free regime I allowed myself to lust only after rock stars and actors. Reverting to virginal adolescent habits seemed a good way to cope with premature celibacy. Because, really, you should be spending your twenties shagging your ass off, it's almost like an obligation.

Love with regular guys had done me no good—and none of them came close to the firecracker love-of-my-life Sullivan. We rolled around for two years. It had been three years since we stopped. By the standard mathematical equations for healing, I had now spent more time without him than with him and so was scientifically guaranteed to be over him. Hallelujah. Though the fact that no one excited me as much as him, since him, worried me. It kept me up late when I wanted to have a dark and brooding night with red wine and Jacques Brel crooning about settling for being the shadow of someone's dog.

Our Bern Baby Bern operation was conceived because Finn was constantly trying to impress Isobel. Isobel adored me like I adored her, and we all loved Dan Bern. She and I had discovered him together, smoking doobies and listening to CJSR one Monday afternoon a few years back. As all three of us were arts graduates with no serious career prospects, the idea of being rock journalists was obviously appealing. Plus, Finn had actually majored in journalism. Isobel had vague notions of fame herself and viewed any opportunity for hanging out with celebrities as good research. I saw the operation as an emotional dress rehearsal for my eventual encounter with Hawksley Workman, my most poetic hero. I believed he would be my soulmate once he had the chance to meet me. Hawksley would forever cure me of any residual Sullivan-ness in my head and heart. I chose him because he had somehow psychically mined my soul to write his lyrics, like we'd been cross-pollinated in the wildflower fields of love. My latest journal entry about him:

> Sweat drops flew off his taut body. His curly black hair was slick with more sweat. His stubble pricked out of his face like a forest around his strawberry-red lips. His pirate earring shone as he belted out his flirtatious lyrics. My whole body vibrated with his sounds. I am madly in love with this gorgeous, sexy-ass troubadour of an incredible male. He is almost too sexy, his lyrics too romantic for me to bear. And as he clutched his mike and sang the last line giving it all the air left in his body I felt all woozy and lightheaded. And then I swear to God he looked right at me with his sultry eyes. Right at *me*!!!!

He kept looking right at me as he dragged out that last note . . .

And then it was all over, five encores was enough and he wasn't coming back from behind the stage. The long-haired roadies were grabbing the instruments and setting up for the next act. I was so excited, so bursting, so high, so . . . I ran to the Sidetrack's bathroom as fast as I could, barely making it before I barfed up that Kraft Dinner and everything else I'd eaten that day.

Since that gig, since that look we shared, and since that portentous vomiting—I have a feeling about Hawksley and me. It's goddamn cosmic.

Getting back to capers: since Isobel and I hit our almost mid-twenties it seemed to me there'd been a shortage of them. We no longer tripped on mushrooms through the streets in the middle of the night or gallivanted around water fountains, stealing statues of Virgin Marys to put in our living rooms. Seemed like mostly what we did now was watch movies and watch other people have way more fun than us. Granted, I loved our times on my couch. We called it the Cadillac. It was vintage '50s: navy velour upholstery, shaped like a spaceship from *The Jetsons*, with stumpy wooden brown conical legs. I got it for twenty-five bucks at the Salvation Army on the north side of the river one lucky Saturday.

Eating popcorn and chocolate. Smoking smokes, drinking diet pop. Everything happened on the Cadillac. What larks! But like Bob Geldof asked in one of my favourite books—his autobiography *Is that It?*—was that it?

I wanted to camp. I wanted to travel on the back of motorcycles and truck cabs. I wanted to have sex under waterfalls with exotic men with tanned bums. I wanted to make movies, paint pictures, go on road trips, have hot affairs in hot-air balloons. Living, not watching. I had extended fantasies of making unforgettable movies, operas, ballets. I had all sorts of enthusiasm but no focus or obvious talent. If it weren't for Cadillac-induced inertia, I was convinced I could participate somehow.

Music was my religion.

More than movies. More than romance. When I went to gigs and watched musicians, I felt the bass in my loins, the melody soaring in my chest, harmonies in my heart. I shared their high as they belted out their lyrics, shook their hair, and thrashed their guitars. I felt so connected at last to humanity.

And all I really wanted in life was to "only connect," like E.M. Forster wrote.

I got this euphoric relief, reprieve, from feeling alone and existential, from staring at the lonely abyss. Life with a soundtrack was so much better than without. So from my perspective, boys with guitars were the luckiest people on earth. I lapped up what they strummed and I wanted more and more while their hands galloped to musical Nirvana. But I didn't know an arpeggio from an armadillo—I was doomed to be forever a fan, not a player.

Music was also my medicine.

I needed some strong medicine post-Sullivan. Something to make me forget how he had claimed the soft places on my body with his lips on those hot August days we floated naked on lilos around our own private lake in southern

Alberta. More than drugs and drink and smoking cigarettes and more than sex, I needed new music. Dan Bern and the others were a salve. They sang about angst like mine, universal love angst, and elevated it to a thing of glory and beauty. When I saw Bern play for the first time the year before at the Sidetrack Café, I felt queasy. After his twelve-song set I had to go outside to get some air. He was full of irony and rebellion and big-time boner sex appeal.

It wasn't just me, the music press had been all over him: likening him to Dylan, the Ghandi of Folk, a gift from Iowa. So when I heard he was coming to town for the annual Edmonton Folk Festival I was practically delirious with lip-smacking anticipation. Isobel and I had rhapsodized for so long about him that Finn used his limited connections, from his intern experience at a Toronto magazine called *Tilt*, to wandangle us an interview.

It was true that Finn had genuine rock journalism ambitions, but the lengths he was prepared to go to orchestrate such a potentially massively embarrassing stunt impressed me. I felt a little guilt over the fact that by pleasing me, I knew he knew he was somehow pleasing Isobel.

"We could meet him, I mean, why the heck not? No, really . . . we'll get an interview," he told us the week before the Folk Fest.

"Ça va pas arriver. Pas possible," Isobel warned. I half believed he might come through though. The month before he'd grown a beard after Isobel casually observed that all intelligent men had beards. Plus he was always threatening to dye his hair blond and have it straightened so he could look like George Emmerson in *A Room with a View*.

Earlier That Day
Saturday Morning, Edmonton Folk Festival
+25 Celsius, blue and cloudless = full-on big prairie sky
mosquito alert = big batch of little fuckers, big but slow

8:00 AM: We waited on the exit side of the entry gate. We hadn't arranged for the press passes early enough to get them by mail, so we had to wait for the girl to find the girl who knew the guy who talked to the girl about our *Tilt* passes. We were the Three Stooges.

9:30 AM: "LADIES, we are in the GATE! Woowee, these press passes are SWANKY," Finn said. "Now, Annie, if you feel faint or nauseous, let us know, babe."

"Finn, I'm sorry, but I think you should perhaps tone it down un p'tit peu," Isobel said, demonstrating lower volume with a hand gesture.

I would never have had the nerve to say it. But it was true, his loudness could blow our cover. Before he had time to feel wounded, we high-fived to celebrate free entry onto the grounds.

I felt mighty in my new persona as big-city press photographer. Isobel seemed to be relishing her role as enigmatic assistant, and Finn, I think he was running on nerves spiked by gasoline. Like if I smoked too near him, he might combust.

We made our way down grassy Gallagher Hill, toward the depths of the city's river valley. We wove our way around the hundreds of blue, yellow, and orange tarps, Mexican blankets, plastic flower markers, backpacks, rainbow-coloured tents, camping chairs, coolers, stoners lying on their backs making daisy chains, and hippie toddlers dancing in the buff. It was a steep hill, so you had to navigate strategically, walking down switchback-style, like a goat. In winter it was a ski hill. Our descent was toughest for Isobel, who was wearing high-heeled wedge sandals—her response to Birkenstock fever.

"Look, j'arrive and this is as political as I get," she said when I complained she was slowing us down with her glamour.

On a good festival weekend, the hill could seat up to ten thousand Edmontonians. This one was cracking up to be a big one, with not just Dan Bern, but Elvis Costello headlining and Joan Baez and loads of African bands in the mix. Mainstage was at the bottom of the hill, which meant every seat had a good view of not just the stage but also of the strong and steady North Saskatchewan River below, with the city's downtown skyline framing the whole vista. As we walked through the crowds, I told Iz, "I hope we don't make such asses out of ourselves that we have to leave town and never come back— I'd miss this festival too much!"

"I know. It's great, isn't it? The cute boy-to-girl ratio is unparalleled."

Fiddlers, drummers, dulcimer, washboard and spoon players, viola aficionados, steel guitarists, and big names from all around the world collided in a musical jamboree for three and a half days every August. Here at the Folk Fest, our city reached heights of coolness that it never matched the rest of the year; except maybe during the odd gig at the New City Likwid Lounge or the Sidetrack Café. It was the one time of year when Isobel and I didn't talk about moving away for good. Edmonton was the kind of place that most young people longed to leave (like New Zealand but without the epic beauty). But in this parkland of grassy fields, balsam poplars, trembling aspen, and eastern cottonwood trees, muddy hills and multiple tents, a kind of utopia exploded every summer.

Everyone remembered the years when it rained too much and the hill morphed into a mass of slip-sliding muddy mayhem. But today was looking like a perfect Big Sky Alberta day. Even though it was still early morning, most of the prime spots for sitting were already taken; the hill looked like a patchwork quilt in progress. I'd never made it up that early, but I'd heard that the tarp run happened every morning at sunrise. Once the gates opened, super-keen folkfesters charged down the hill, toppling over one another, doing accidental roly-polys to get the prime locations for stargazing. We laid our tarp on some free grass mid-hill to the far left of mainstage, beside a wholesome-looking family who seemed like they would defend our tarp and maybe share snacks.

There were families who had been coming for twenty-five years, since the very first festival. Singing "Four Strong Winds" on closing night at the top of your lungs was practically a universal Edmonton experience. Once you got past the mosquitoes, toxic porta-potties, mud, and patchouli miasma, the Edmonton Folk Fest was the best of its kind Canada-wide. Admittedly Vancouver had the ocean, and the North Country Fair in northern Alberta had the homegrown, middle-of-nowhere bonus, but E-town really had the perfect combination of river valley, prairie sky, and grassy hills.

The beer garden, a central feature, was a cordoned-off section of the park with picnic benches and canopies, for shelter from sun or rain, where you plowed through beer and scoped cuties. The danger was going in for one and then staying there all weekend and never seeing any music. Two beers into our first beer garden shift we perfected our plan. Finn was the chief of operations. An unassuming CEO, he was endearing in his standard gear: a New York Rangers baseball cap, vintage

Hawaiian shirt, ginger stubble, and freckles. His plan was two-pronged: 1) impromptu all the way 2) imagine we are Hunter S., Annie Leibovitz, and Tallulah Bankhead (H.A.T.). Isobel's role was clearly the best: she just exuded her natural air of importance and decadence.

9:35 AM: We reported to the sterile, khaki, safari-looking media tent. In my pre-interview day scenario-izing I had envisioned a gigantic tent full of press people milling about, where nobody would notice me and my straw hat. But this tent was the kind you go camping in with your boyfriend (maybe) and dog (possibly), if it was a small dog, or small boyfriend, for that matter. The tent was full of hardcore types, looking like foreign war correspondents in their khaki multi-pocket pants and utility vests carrying tripods, bipods, pods, and fifteen hundred lenses. They were screamingly legitimate-looking. It must have been the khaki. Us though—the Bern Baby Bern Operation, with my orange overall shorts, blue bandana around my neck, and general ironic cowgirl chic and Isobel's high-heel disaster—looked at worst like hacks from a small-town weekly or at best university journalists (neither would garner a lot of respect from the Khakis). We hadn't scripted anything beforehand, having agreed we would leave it all to our natural wit and alcohol.

The only reason I was pretending to be the photographer and Finn got to be the writer was because I might suffer from stress muteness during the interview. Finn, after all, had actually worked for a real magazine, and Isobel didn't have a nerve problem. To calm down and stop myself from flailing my arms in anticipation, I strolled around the tent while Finn lined up to talk to the coordinator girl with the hippie skirt. Isobel got busy looking bored and sexy. Unfortunately a lap took almost no time in this pup tent—if I circled more than three times, they were going to think I had a disorder of some kind—so I concentrated on looking serious, ready to speak journo at any point. As I stared at a map of the river valley, Finn stepped up to bat.

"Finn Hingley, PLEASED TO MEET YOU. JOHN, from *Tilt* in Torono, got in touch with CINDY last week and told her he'd be sending myself, my colleague, and my photographer to do a think-piece on DAN BERN."

Coordinator Girl: "Hi, I'm Ursula . . . Ya, I think I saw you on the list . . . so, you guys from TO?" I could recognize a bit of that small-town defensiveness that all we E-towners have.

"YUP, JUST FLEW IN."

"Great, well, just pick a time on the board where that girl with the huge hat is and sign up. I think he still has a slot open."

When I looked under Dan Bern's name, every slot was checked off; he was full for the day. I felt winded by the blow. Finn came up beside me and smiled like I was a stranger. He saw the look of despair on my face, looked at the board, and lightning fast he grabbed the Jiffy marker and made a whole new row. He wrote *Tilt Magazine, Toronto* and put two serious-looking asterisks beside it. We now had the new last opening of the day.

He walked back over to the girl and reached out his hand to shake hers. "Hey, thanks a lot, we really appreciate the last-minute thing—YOU'RE DOING A GREAT JOB HERE. Are you going to be able to catch Bern's set? You really should, ya know."

"No, I doubt it, I'm committed to Stage 5. Ron Sexsmith. Same timeslot, you know how it is. But, uh, listen, do you have a card or a copy of the mag?"

"OH SHIT . . ." He slapped himself on the forehead. "No . . . sorry, they screwed up with our luggage at the airport. But we'll send the Folk Fest office a copy of the issue when it comes out. Should I forward it to your attention?"

It was a good recovery, but Finn was right, we should've picked up a copy at 7-Eleven. Was that skepticism in her eyes? Did she know? Would she tell?

We exited the tent one at a time, so as to not look too eager. As soon as we were out of her sight line we high-fived it one more time. The gesture was starting to become a compulsive thing, our collective nervous tic.

10:00 AM–2:00 PM-ish: The three of us spent the sunny hours roaming the grounds, checking out workshops. Each of us wore unusually large black sunglasses just in case we'd bump into people who might blow our cover by accident. Between Isobel and me, we probably knew half of Edmonton, so we had no alternative but to snub people. We had to focus on our mission. I was convinced the coordinator girl was going to get on her walkie-talkie and then some Security Guy with cartoon Popeye muscles and a fog horn was gonna start yelling in front of all of Edmonton: "STOP THOSE FAKES, THEY'RE NOT FROM TORONTO; THEY'RE NOT REAL JOURNALISTS; TWO OF THEM WORK AT RIGOLETTO'S DOWNTOWN AND THE OTHER ONE IS UNEMPLOYED!" We'd be hopelessly exposed. The trauma, the trauma . . .

Dan's afternoon show on Stage 4 was a raging success. Midway through his concert, he had the whole crowded hill giving him a standing ovation. His song "True Revolutionaries" was the big hit.

15

And in Berkeley
And in Greenwich Village
And in Paris
And in Scottsbluff, Nebraska
No one sits around funky little coffee shops
    anymore
Talking revolution
They get a Starbucks to go
They go back to their basketball games
Where they see who can jump higher
Who can jam
Who can take it to the rack
And they all wear baseball caps
'Cept they don't say Yankees or Dodgers or
    Cardinals anymore
They say Nike; Reebok; Adidas
Because the pro players don't play for teams
    anymore
They play for shoe companies

I was so happy to see him play again. It rebustled my
spirit. The man could give you shivers one note in. He was
a new kind of protest singer, not corny, not overly earnest,
but wry and swaggering. He juggled songs about baseball
with ones about Henry Miller and Van Gogh. He navigated a
fusion between literary and macho sports stuff. He wasn't just
a set of gorgeous biceps; the man could think and had obviously read some books. But it was his next song, "Jerusalem"
that sent me off the deep end and straight to the ground,
unconscious.

2:30 PM: Back on my feet, I was revived, the fainting episode way behind me—three Big Rocks inside me. Isobel was off buying jewellery and summer dresses she didn't need in the big tent while I stooged out back in the beer garden and Blue Rodeo sweetly played mountain love songs on the mainstage. There were speakers in the tent, so you wouldn't miss the music if you were stuck there. Under the feverish sun, sky-high poplar treetops gave us serene shady spots. Five flavours of beer flowed non-stop from keg spouts into pitchers and plastic glasses. Happy people puttered about, like children on the beach. You could hear a hum of "ahhhh": the rapture of the beer garden scene. Collective contentment that was the essence of the folk festival—never-ending good times. A fuzzy, sunshine beery haze eclipsed my paranoia. I pointed my face up at the sun—to hell with the danger—my skin drank the sunbeams and I felt warm all through my chest and heart, legs and toes. I looked at the inside skin of my eyelids and dwelled in the orange until I felt like I was inside a tangerine. I forgot about my towering student loans, my nerve problem, my fainting issue, my lack of direction, Sullivan. Gorging on music and sunshine, what could be better?! Plus, I was going to interview Dan Bern later.

3:50 PM: Fearless Finn was off getting Dan Bern, and I was sitting alone at a picnic bench, as far away as possible from other beer garden dwellers. I was scared back into sobriety and felt a little dizzy from all the sun. Plus I had tumultuous guts—intestines gurgling in waves of fraudulence all the while writhing with small bubbles of righteousness—I was a freelance writer—I wrote (in my journal) and I was free. Ya! Granted I wasn't a photographer and *Tilt* didn't specifically commission Finn to cover this piece. But, I mean, c'mon: "the survival of folk music in an increasingly electronic/ironic age," it was a totally plausible hook, even if a little pretentious.

3:51 PM: I was starting to doubt that we were actually doing this. My body couldn't help but to express my disbelief; my fidgeting was getting out of hand. I wrestled with my postures. I couldn't decide if I should put my bag on the table, take out the camera, hold a pen, have a smoke, scratch my head, look in a mirror to make sure I didn't have any green onion cake stuck in my teeth. I fixated on my hair, making sure my badly positioned cowlick right at the top of my skull wasn't doing its standing ovation. Before I could censor myself, I dipped my finger in my beer and tried to flatten the rogue strands. I wondered if the Princess Leia hairdo was a good choice for today.

I objected to that *groupie* word. Guys didn't get called groupies, *fan* was a much better tag. I think the first big crazy fans were those bobby-soxers who went goofy over Frank Sinatra. I guess I must be a descendant of that tribe. But at least I wasn't like those nutbars on Bern's website; those people were rabid. It's just like he explained in his "Abduction" song. After he returns home from the alien spaceship where he'd been abducted, he sang:

> Well, my life's back to normal now
> I do the things I always do
> 'Cept once a week I meet with 12
> Other folks who've been abducted too
> I tell my story
> They tell theirs
> I don't believe them, though

3:53 PM: What if someone came to sit down? This was

exhausting. I needed to prepare, dammit. Should I take out my pens and paper? Despite the nerves, I had a feeling that I would look back on this as a great adventure as soon as it was over. I was already looking forward to being nostalgic. This was my first caper for ages as far I could remember—barring those you have on a smoked salmon pizza.

Just then I caught sight of the last person in the world I wanted to see. I squinted.

Not him . . .

Shittttt.

Better hide, I couldn't explain that I was suddenly a photographer. Bern Baby Bern hadn't properly accounted for civilian sightings.

Why did he always look so good?

I suppose he wasn't everybody's type. His tanned skin, his slender toes poking out of his ratty tennis shoes, his wild dark eyes and longish floppy black hair that usually smelled of campfire smoke. It was his eyes that got you. Sultry, come-fuck-me eyes.

I bent down to tie my shoe. I realized I had no laces, so I stroked a couple of blades of grass.

"Hey, Annie, how's it going?"

"Fantastic."

"You enjoying yourself? Seen any good bands?"

"Ya."

He looked at me, weirdly, and I wondered if there was any possible way he could know what I was up to.

"That's a pretty fancy camera you got there?"

"Uh, well . . . actually, ya . . . I'm kind of a rock journalist . . . photographer . . . for the day anyway, you know . . ."

"Really? Cool . . . How did that happen?"

"I gotta pee."

4:00 PM: I hid by a falafel tent for a while. I just wanted to be cool. This had the makings of being pretty cool. I think Sullivan probably noticed how cool I was with all my gear. Or maybe really lame. We were behaving like total weirdoes. Everyone else was happily sitting on their ass watching music. But us, we were in the heart of the action. Maybe Dan would notice how cool I was and we could hang out and I don't know, maybe I'd find something to do on the tour bus when he was gigging. I could be a real photographer. The technical side of cameras always buffaloed me, but I was excellent with a Polaroid. Point and shoot, baby, point and shoot!

I was sweating with the strain of trying to look casual and relaxed and natural. Should I go check my hair? There were no mirrors in the porta-potties. Where was Isobel? I lit another smoke, and put a mint in my mouth to counteract tobacco breath, then worried about the combination giving me mouth cancer. In a worried blur I watched the falafel man roll his little dumpling balls and drop them into the deep fryer one after another like a Zen master.

God, Finn was brave. Isobel was brilliant too, not being at all nervous. There must have been something wrong with me to be so nervous. It was hard to believe we were going to actually meet him. For real.

I knew I shouldn't keep thinking I'm nervous. I'm nervous. I'm really really nervous. Nervous nervousnervousnervousnervousnerrrrrrrrrrvususususus us nerve us. What did it mean . . . nerve us?

I was looking at myself in my pocket mirror every couple of minutes. This happens when I panic, I start to feel at odds with my body. Like my soul is floating away. Badly attached.

Disembodied. However you want to call it, I stare and stare at myself trying to attach the image to my soul. It's not an easy fit.

I changed my mantra to: I'm calm. I'm relaxed. I'm super cool and super suave and what . . . the hell is that? Bird shit on my sleeve?

That is so unattractive.

I walked back to the Bern Baby Bern headquarters picnic bench, which was miraculously free. Sullivan was nowhere in the vicinity. I pulled out the novel I was packing, *Ana Karenina*, my favourite love story after *A Room with a View*. It was a bit tragic with her pelting herself on the train tracks, but boy oh boy was it romantic.

4:00 PM-ish: "Hey," said Isobel just as I was contemplating potential exits. I could see myself taking the fence if I took a running leap. Meeting a hero really wasn't for the meek.

"Tell me when they're coming, I can't look," I said and put on my big glasses again.

"C'est vraiment dommage they don't serve Kir Royales here. I mean, a little bubbly would be parfait in this setting . . . Oh look, ils sont là bas. ETA: une minute. Is that bird kaka on your shirt?" Isobel asked. "Don't worry, this is just like the time we did that stakeout when I was trying to seduce that Ukrainian guy, do you souviens? What was his code name, Ski?"

It's true, we did have a bit of a history of stakeouts and harmless stalking. Accidentally bumping into people was my personal specialty. But I couldn't muster any of the nonchalance I needed for this. Man, I wished I was up on the hill, stoned and happily watching Blue Rodeo. I felt nauseated.

But I couldn't abandon Finn.

More than anything, I wanted desperately to go home to my couch and my fuzzy blanket. But I was stuck, the only thing I could do was act completely disinterested as I watched Finn walk up to the table with Dan Bern.

Mister Dan Bern.

I pretended to fiddle with a camera lens; I took another gulp of beer.

He was right in front of me.

He wasn't your average lanky rock star, he was big and had peachy-tanned guitar-muscled arms, angel-food-cake-blond-coloured hair, stubbly face. He was gorgeous in a Californian surfer dude kind of way. I looked over at Finn; he looked unbearably nervous. You could almost see individual nerves dancing just beneath his skin. Finn sat down, and Dan headed to the porta-potties for the pre-interview pee.

"Oh man, it's not going well, is it," I said, noticing the hundreds of crazy sweat bubbles reproducing by the minute on Finn's forehead.

"Shite . . . he's not very talkative. I gave him the *Tilt* spiel on the way over and all I got was uh-huhs. We got really confused because he thought I said Spliff instead of *Tilt*."

I realized then how terrible it could be—the full scope of the horror. If Finn couldn't charm him, we were hooped.

Not having a proper strategy was moronic. We weren't improv veterans.

Isobel got up and dashed off. She was too fast for me, though I considered trying to lasso her with my bag strap.

Dan ambled back over to the table. He looked like he was dreading it.

"Dan Bern, this is Annie Jones, photographer for *Tilt Magazine*."

"Hi. I'm a big fan," I said, standing up and sticking out my hand, knowing it was probably clammy.

"Hey," he said, shaking my hand.

Did I feel an antagonistic vibe?

"Let's sit," Finn said.

I poured us four pints of Big Rock from the pitcher and pressed play on my professional-looking little tape recorder.

"Who's the fourth beer for? Do y'all have like, I dunno, an invisible friend or somethin?" Dan joked.

Finn and I laughed way too loudly. It was a horrible, staccato burst: HA HA HA HA.

We looked at each other and stopped laughing.

Then it was all silent except for the angry wasp circling my beer.

I couldn't possibly start the interview, so I gave Finn what I hoped was a serious, let's-get-to-work kind of a nod.

"Ya, our colleague just went missing. But we don't want to waste your time, so we'll get started. So, uh, what do you think about protest songs in this day and age, it seems like the only way they can happen is if they're ironic, why is that? Like your song 'True Revolutionaries,' it's *great*, but is it the audience that changes the interpretation of it or is it you? I don't know . . . I don't know," said Finn, looking confused but earnest.

There was a bad-tasting silence as Dan looked at him quizzically, cocking his head sideways, like a dog that's perplexed.

The awkwardness was reaching toxic levels.

". . . I don't know what you're asking . . ." Dan finally answered.

"Ya, me neither, man, sorry about that . . ." Finn replied quickly, sweating some more, eyes shifting back and forth.

Thank God! Gorgeous Isobel with her honey-brown skin and Lake Louise green eyes was back at the table with a baggie full of those little sugary doughnuts that no one is immune to—seductive golden nuggets of deep-fried lardy dough sprinkled with sweet crystals.

Finn and Dan looked at her like she was an angel. Finn announced, "This is my colleague, Isobel Sparks. She's our doughnut supplier . . ."

"That was very rude of me. We need to keep Annie's blood sugar up, and I thought I could get back in time, but I got waylaid by the crowds headed to the bathing pool." Isobel laughed.

"I sure hate it when I get waylaid." Dan laughed back. He looked sexy. It was a bit painful for me (the flirty winds not blowing in my direction but hers), but the vibe seemed to have instantly gotten better—*flirting more potent than beer*, I scribbled in my notebook.

Stuffing a couple doughnuts in my mouth, I glimpsed the Coordinator Girl checking us out with a look on her face that could mean we were busted.

"So what were we talking about?" Isobel asked.

"You know, folk music thriving in an increasingly electronic age," Finn said.

"Oh, that's tedious. Let's get to the more interesting stuff, like . . . I don't know . . . what kind of underwear do you prefer wearing?" Isobel said, laughing at her own humour.

"Well that depends. Mostly boxers, cotton ones. But I hate to say it, lately I've been going through a commando phase, particularly in the warmer months. But then . . ."

"Right, right, that's great. But uh, Isobel, we do have to give *Tilt* what they want, it's a mag for techies after all." Finn was a little red in the face.

"Yes, yes, sorry. Finn can't write a story about underwear. Mind you, I think somebody should write something about thongs, they are truly absurd." Isobel laughed some more. I was in awe of her boldness. "Why don't you tell us some stories about being on the road. What's it like being a rock star? What kind of gossip do you got?" she asked in a mock Barbara Walters tone.

Dan smiled coyly at Isobel. She always knew how to play it right.

"I don't got a lot of gossip. I'm a guy, for freakin' sakes. We don't talk about shit. We grunt. We watch sports. We talk sports. Sometimes we talk about chicks, but it's kind of like talking about cars. I hate to tell y'all, but the stereotypes are true."

"There's no myth more appealing to girls than a bad-ass with a golden heart. I don't believe what they say about musicians—you can't tell me they're all cheating, lying sons-o-bitches. How could they sing all those love songs then?" This was a subject so close to my heart, it was practically sitting on it. Finn, Isobel, and Dan Bern looked at me like I was on drugs.

"Look, I just started playing music so I could score some chicks! I'm sorry—it's true, and almost every other guy musician I know is the same," Dan said.

It was a good time to get more beer. Even if I wasn't doing so well as an interviewer, the most important thing was that our Subject was warming up, loosening. I walked over to the beer pourers. From the lineup, I could see the back of the Coordinator Girl's purple tie-dyed T-shirt. She was talking to one of those crew people with the shirts that read: SECURITY. He turned around to look at our gang. I steered myself and the beer quickly back to the table. Surely they wouldn't interrupt us mid-interview.

When I got back to the table, I topped up everyone's beer and then circled the table, pretending to take some arty pictures. At one point, I squatted and realized I was actually aiming the camera at Dan's thighs, which looked pretty luscious at that angle. I snapped the picture quickly, feeling a little self-loathing over objectifying the guy.

I got up to take some less demeaning shots. As I clicked away, it seemed like the rapport at the table was growing.

But the Coordinator Girl was holding her position.

"How do you make that eeenn eeen waaah noise?" Finn asked while air-guitaring.

"Funny you should notice that, that's a new technique I'm working on. It's kind of like a combo slide/hammer pluck," Dan said, demonstrating with his fingers on his own air guitar.

Isobel took hold of the conversation again: "How long have you been playing?"

"I've been playing since . . . I play all the time, since I was a little kid, thank God I didn't forget how. Do you play?" Dan asked Isobel.

She shook her head no. Dan continued, "Not at all? You never play?"

"Music?" Isobel asked, arching an eyebrow coquettishly.

Oh God help us. This was nauseating. I looked over at Finn, he winked. He was squirming too. I looked over to where I'd last seen the Coordinator Girl. She'd moved. She could be anywhere.

"Oh ya, I play," Isobel replied.

"Well okay then, gotta play!" Dan smirked and took a gulp of beer.

Disgusting—they were raunchy flirters.

Being a journalist is a cinch, I thought for a fleeting second, but then the Coordinator Girl came back into my range of vision. But she was smooching the security guy! Like full-on power necking. Maybe we were off the hook. I stopped holding my breath.

"Enough of all this heavy talk. Now, seriously, tell me what level of hedonism are we talking about on tour?" Finn asked.

"How hard do I party, is that what you are asking?" Dan laughed.

"Like on a scale of one to ten, one being Cliff Richard and ten being Keith Richards, who I heard gets his whole blood supply replaced every now and then so he can survive his debauchery," Finn explained.

"I . . . well . . . I guess I'd be around a five . . . maybe seven. You know it's hard work, touring, you gotta be healthy. You can't just be a drunken bum like people think. Not at my humble level of success anyway. When you get to be mega big, then maybe you can have people schlepp you around. Fly you in and out of cities. You can be wasted if you're flying first class and staying at like the Schmilton or whatever. But me, I gotta get myself places. So that means mostly being straight," Dan said, helping himself to the beer.

"Well, I think the formal part of our interview is done. Do you want to hang out and have beers? I could get another pitcher," Finn offered.

"That'd be thoughtful," Dan accepted.

Finn went on a beer run, and I took some photos of Dan by himself and then some with Isobel, who took advantage of the situation by posing with her arm thrown casually around his neck.

"Hey, let me wear some of those goofy sunglasses you've all

got. What's up with them anyway, makes y'all look like you're in a cult," Dan said.

I gave him my glasses even though they were holding my hair in place. He slid them on. They didn't look too bad on him. "These glasses smell like beer. What did you do, stick your head in a keg?" Dan and Isobel laughed. I tried to imagine I was delightful like Annie Hall: sexy goofy. Finn came back from the booze run with beer and armfuls of green onion cakes.

I loved green onion cakes. They were like pancakes with onions. Greasy dough with a savoury flavour. My teeth sank in to the sticky dough, oil seeped into my mouth. All of it triggering the happy chemicals in my brain.

Then Finn launched one of his classic Finnisms: "So when you're touring in foreign countries, is it a truer you that you present to people, or just another mythology . . . I mean, that's what everyone does, we create myths around ourselves and then when we go travelling . . . we can totally reinvent ourselves, make up new myths, d'ya know what I mean?"

"I don't think those myths are wrong though . . ." Dan somehow clicked with Finn's babbling.

"No, man, they're not wrong, you gotta have 'em, you gotta live, you gotta get through the day."

In my mind I screamed to Finn, "NOW'S NOT THE TIME TO REVEAL OUR JOURNALISM MYTH, DON'T DO IT, HE'S NOT READY!"

"Even beyond getting through the day, I mean, I think . . . I think those myths are real," Dan repeated.

"They have to be . . ." Finn agreed with beery passion. I think Finn clung to a lot of personal myths. Like he was destined to be Canada's Hunter S. Thompson; Isobel was sure to fall in love with him once she understood his true genius; he would become a hugely sought-after singer-songwriter, and foreign correspondent. We had often talked dreams/myths after work at the restaurant, unwinding over a few Heinekens or Gin Talkings, as we liked to call them.

I think we had reached our goal. The mood was great, or at least relaxed. We were palling around with Dan Bern and he was flirting with Isobel.

6:05 PM: The tape recorder clicked off. I was a little tipsy. We babbled some more about everything. I think we covered Woody Guthrie, High School, Tennis, Why Canada Is Fabulous, Bad Journalists' Questions, his defence of Henry Miller, both Elvises, New York Pedestrians, Jaywalking in Alberta, Sunglasses, Dogs, and all of our astrological signs. Blue Rodeo had long finished playing, and Gillian Welch was starting up when Dan finally said, "I gotta get back 'cause I'm drunk."

7:30 PM: After expending all that nervous energy, I was tired but feeling relatively normal about the whole thing.

"Guys, maybe we should take on Costello! Or Bowie, I think he's on tour somewhere. We could go on the road!" Finn enthused. "It's like that Woody Allen line about the world opening up for us like one big vagina!!!"

"Easy there, chief . . . A road trip, ya, that would be dreamy. I could use a holiday . . ." I said.

Isobel kept mumbling to both of our annoyances how charmant Bern was. He had scribbled his email address on her arm in Jiffy blue permanent ink. We'd have to see it for a while yet.

We climbed the hill later and sacked out on the tarp, ready for the candle-lit portion of the evening. Everyone brought candles to light at twilight. There was even a procession of kids walking down the hill with flickering paper lanterns held aloft. Festivals are so much better than stadium concerts; there's just no contest. As we lay back and listened to the tunes, a feeling of widespread goodwill swept the hill and I revelled in Edmonton at its most magical. Isobel was letting Finn rub her feet. Even though I saw Sullivan sitting farther down the hill with his freaky tall new girlfriend wrapped around him, I sang along to "Four Strong Winds," thinking this day had turned into the kind you knew you would never forget. A real Top 10 day.

The rest of the festival was a perfect lost weekend of booze, more green onion cakes with atomically hot sauce, doughnuts, smiles to cute boys, flirtations in the porta-potty lineup, and great tunes. After the weekend we were left ravaged, exhausted, and gastrointestinally challenged but happified. Mostly though we were very proud of our stunt. Finn especially felt like the King of the World. And I began to think of another quest being possible: maybe Hawksley and I could meet sooner than I thought. It might be time to meet him, in the flesh. What flesh. Mmmm

"Too much love is like too much dope
First you laugh then you choke
We were a tug of war with too much rope
We got covered in mud, then the rope just broke
But ooh wah baby I'll think of you
I'm sure to laugh, and cry a little too
Boo hoo hoo"

"Ooh Wah Baby," Ben Sures

A week later I was sitting in the window seat at the Sugar Bowl coffee shop on the south side of the river, savouring a buttery sweet cinnamon bun, layer by layer, drinking a black cup of coffee, and looking at a road atlas when I noticed Finn, looking a bit apocalyptic, crossing the room toward me through the late afternoon sunshine haze. Jazzy ska horns trumpeted from the speakers as he jostled with the palm tree and chairs in his path. I examined him, wondering yet again how Isobel managed to hook-line-and-sink so many good-quality guys. Since the festival stunt he had thought he'd impressed Isobel so much she'd go out with him for ages. He didn't know of the long history of stuntmen in her past, and it didn't serve him that he was one of the sweetest.

When he got up close to my table, I could see he had a large wet stain covering the outside of his left leg. It looked like he had stepped into a puddle up to his knee.

"Hi, how are you doing? What's that you're reading? Are you planning a trip?" Compared to his normal sound level, he was practically whispering. I handed him the atlas that I was marking up with possible routes.

"We're thinking of going to Montreal next week."

"Right. So, uh, listen, have you seen her lately?"

"We met up for a late breakfast."

"Oh, did she . . . ?"

"Look, Finn, what can I tell ya—"

"Oh don't worry, I'm totally fine. Totally. I just . . . well, you know. I just really think she's great." He smiled helplessly, and I wondered why he thought she was so great if she had just given him the boot.

Something didn't smell so good, a bit like parmesan cheese. I looked around at the food on people's tables wondering which one it was coming from. From the speakers Tom Waits growled some cacophony about a guy named Frank and some raining dogs and steaming gutters.

"You know you really shouldn't take it too personally. It's truly not about you. She's fickle, flirty, capricious, whatever you want to call it."

"Ya she's like the wind . . . 'Wild is the Wind,' you know that Bowie song?"

"I love Nina Simone's version too."

"So I probably shouldn't call her, should I? I mean, I would just like to tell her I'm fine and maybe we could go for lunch."

"I don't think—"

He got up quickly, his springy curls bouncing as he walked over to the payphone on the wall beside the condiments counter. I watched him plug in his quarter and prod the numbers enthusiastically. He tilted his head to the left and sandwiched the phone between his neck and shoulder. With his left hand he lit a cigarette. He had one hand free to gesticulate; he was one of those people who really talked with his hands. The call lasted about one single minute. He looked at the phone for a moment before hanging up. He slouched back over to the table, dragging his feet, defeat in his eyes. My stomach spasmed, the cinnamon roll sat uncomfortably in my guts. I remembered how it was when Sullivan left. That pure disbelief that he could actually just go. Be gone from me. All my privileges taken away.

"You know what . . . I . . . I'm fine. I'm glad I did that."

There was no escaping this: he needed help. "Finn, what happened?"

"D'ya really wanna know?"

"Tell me everything." I sighed quietly, knowing he needed to talk it out. "Let me get a beer first, do you want one?"

"Sure, whatever—"

I went to the counter and got two Heinekens from the cute bartender.

"So I'm sitting at Pizza Hut wondering what I'm doing there. They play boy-band music there, for Chrissakes. It's like a hockey-jock hangout. All these guys are there stuffing their faces with pepperoni and cheese pizzas. Chins everywhere glistening with grease, it's gross, know what I mean? Cheering for the Oilers, mooning the Flames. I can't figure out why Bella wants to meet here. It's part of her charm though, you know, mystery. So anyway, eventually she shows up looking ridiculously foxy, right?"

"Yes."

"I mean, really *hot*. She's wearing this black dress with twelve buttons down the front. I counted them while she was standing at the salad bar, spooning out croutons and bacon bits. And go-go boots."

"What?"

"She was wearing go-go dancer boots up to her thighs."

"Right," I said. I really would've preferred to go home, but Finn was definitely too messy to be left untended.

"So she sits down and asks me first if I remember that this was just supposed to be a casual fling, no strings. And I say yes. And she says, 'So why are you calling me five times a night?' I didn't quite know what to say. It's just that so many things make me think of her, like I was watching TV and I saw this show on penguins and she likes penguins so I had to call her. And then I was making a cup of tea and I noticed that we both like the same kind of peppermint tea and that's cosmic so I called her . . . I know, in retrospect it was ridiculous. I was in way in over my head and I didn't even know it."

I went up to the counter and got us each another beer. The bartender winked at me.

"You're a peach. Thanks for the beer . . . So the funny thing is I was thinkin' I was all casual like, just calling her a few times, but otherwise restraining myself, not getting too heavy, too intense. I limited myself to only two telephone calls a day. And I kept saying to myself: I'm fine. I can handle this. I'm cool. And so today after she told me that we had to stop hanging out I thought again: I'm fine. All the way out the door, I kept thinking how fine I was, I said goodbye, I paid the bill, I left Pizza Hut. I got in my car and I'm driving home down 99th Street, past Barb and Ernie's—you know the German restaurant where the guy wears lederhosen? And just then I vomited down the side of my leg. I vomited! I was surprised as hell because hey: I'm *fine*. I'm *great*. What am I doing puking on my leg? So I manage to pull into a bus stop and open the door, and I puke some more in the gutter! And so . . ."

My stomach heaved. "Oh God, it's not parmesan, it's you! I think maybe you should go put some more soap on that."

Finn went to the men's room armed with Lysol from the bartender. I could feel my eyes starting to tear up, but I had no idea why.

He came out of the bathroom, smelling antiseptic. He was smiling, repeating to himself and me: "I'm fine, really, I'm fine."

"Okay, Finn, listen to me. You are not fine now, but you are going to be fine. Get yourself some supplies. How about some Häagen-Dazs ice cream, pizza, whatever . . . Go home and listen to eight sad songs twice at least—songs like Costello's 'I Want You,' and Brel's 'Ne me Quittes Pas'; listen to Townes' Van Zandt, Nick Drake, whatever you gotta do—and then have a hot bath and cry yourself to sleep. The guys at Blackbyrd Myoozik shop coached me on The Listening Cure and gave me the Van Zandt tip and it's true, he's super sad.

"You'll wake up feeling purged. Drink lots of water, otherwise you're gonna get dehydrated. The night after that read some Sylvia Plath, then watch a couple of wrist-slashers like *Shadowlands*, *Steel Magnolias*, *The Champ*, and cry some more. Movies with lots of bereavement. Call me anytime. The main thing is to get it out of your system, cry it out. Think: Operation Purge. Then watch something like *The Commitments* to reboot yourself."

"Don't you think there's any hope?"

"I wish there was, Finn. I'm trying to be honest. Go home. Do what I say. Call me if you need me. Anytime."

Because I'd seen so many of Isobel's victims in Finn's state, her mankilling had become a sad fact of the universe, like acid rain, so I couldn't really offer much in the way of solace or hope for reconciliation. I decided to hope that he was fine

enough for me to leave him by himself, but I still felt guilty.
I should've given him a heads-up ages ago. I should've, but I
wanted the Dan Bern thing to happen. I sucked.

Later that night, in Isobel's apartment, I threw myself down
on the plum-coloured couch. She handed me a bowl of popcorn and a glass for the red wine on the coffee table. She had a
cozy apartment on the top floor of a three-storey walk-up. Her
one-bedroom suite used to be basic, but she had transformed
it into a loveshack extraordinaire. Arabian fabrics draped
on the slanted wall. A beaded curtain hung in the bedroom
doorway. There was a mosquito net sensually cocooning her
bed, like in *Out of Africa*. Candles floated in water in glass
vases around the apartment. A philodendron's vine circled the
upper part of the four living room walls like a leafy green
necklace. A Virgin Mary icon hung above the hallway arch.
A priest she had tried to seduce had given it to her after she
started showing up too regularly at church events.

"So j'arrive à Pizza Hut, which is terrible as you know,
but I figure I'm relatively anonyme there. So he's all friendly
and everything and I'm feeling mal, because it really is not
fun being the dumper. The dumpee has no guilt whereas la
dumper can barely walk with the load of feeling bad on her
back. T'sais? Anyway, there Finn was, waiting patiently, doing
his crossword puzzle. And so I smile and stuff a cigarette in my
mouth so I don't have to keep fake smiling cause it's exhausting, and he starts in on our summer plans! The guy's fou
totallement fou. I say casual sex, and he says let's go camping
in the peach orchards in Penticton."

"I think he just likes you an awful lot—"

"Bof! The tablecloth was this 'orrible plastic red-and-white faux Italian gingham. I can't stand these franchise restaurants. Anyway, the other customers are cheering every two seconds because Gretzky keeps on scoring. Finn drank a Blue or Pilsner or—"

"I don't need all the details, really." Isobel liked nothing better than to have a good old gossip about the minute events of her daily life.

"C'mon. Don't be like that, I'm trying to give you toute l'histoire. All right, here it is: I looked at him firmly, I didn't blink, and I said three things." Isobel paused.

"What three things?"

"I said: Non. Non. And non. And with each non I pointed my finger at him to punctuate. 'Course he tried to break in:

"'But—'

"'Non.'

"'But—'

"'Noooo.' And then finally he got it."

"So what did you tell him when he called you this afternoon?"

"I repeated the three nons. Apparently all great political speeches come in threes, three words, three slogans. Long Live Peace. We Will Triumph . . . Tu es fini."

She said Finn had called her five times the night before, getting more ridiculous with each call, aiming for casual and landing desperate. It was probably a good thing she had cut him loose after all. She wasn't ready for anything more than a fling. Whenever we went to a movie or a play or got on a bus or plane, she always went straight for aisle seats, always positioned herself near exit signs. Her dad, whose advice on life consisted of sporting clichés, had told her long ago: the only way around the best offence is a good defence. She dumped first—dating survival of the fittest. "Treat 'em mean, keep 'em keen" was practically her mantra.

"You know Finn is a great guy, and he went way out of his way to get us that Dan Bern interview."

"So, what, I'm supposed to commit myself for life to this guy? He wants to be a rock journalist anyway; it was a good experience for him too. I just can't deal with his needs. He's too open, too warm, too . . . goddamn eager."

"Oh," I said, realizing that's probably what Sullivan had thought of me. Too eager. To keep him. To have him stay. No matter how broken we were.

"You look a little funny, darling. You okay?" Isobel asked.

"The guy vomited on his pants. Finn was sick to his stomach," I told her.

"He didn't?"

"He did, when he was driving home from Pizza Hut."

"Oh," she said, and then quoting *A Room with a View*: "'I shall never forgive myself, never to my dying day.'"

She got up to open another bottle of wine.

"I am writing
graffiti on your body,
I am drawing the story
of how hard we tried;
. . . your bones have been my bed frame,
and your flesh has been my pillow
. . . the old woman behind the pink curtains
and the closed door
on the first floor
she's listening through the air shaft
to see how long
our swan song can last . . ."

"Both Hands," Ani DiFranco

The Couch Sessions
Unplugged & Horizontal

The next day I stayed in bed way way too late. Late to the point of self-disgust. No one sleeps like the depressed. It was two in the afternoon when the doorbell rang. All I saw when I opened the door were flowers bursting with happy colour, and lots of them. And some guy's hairy legs under them. His face, hidden by the sheer mass of petals and stalks. They smelled gorgeous.

A delivery of twenty-four yellow-and-plum coloured tiger lilies. At last, I thought, at last. Romance! For me! My heartbeat sped up and my face warmed. I smiled bashfully as if I was at an awards ceremony. The delivery guy looked a bit nervous.

"Uh, I'm sorry, these are for the girl next door. She's not, uh, home. Would you mind keeping them for her?"

I took them in and put them in some water. Good karma, I thought. It really didn't help my mood though. I'd been lying in bed, thinking about Finn, Finn and Sullivan, me and Sullivan. Sullivan and the Amazon girlfriend. Sullivan and Isobel. Fixating in a vortex of Sullivan, I could feel myself going down that dark road, the one I know better than to go down. Sometimes, I can't resist the sick pleasure of it.

I related to Finn more than I wanted to—fellow underdogs of love and all. He was still in the throes of love angst, but I wanted to think I was well beyond all that—Sullivan was ancient news. But it was true that I still did, on dark days, spend hours and sometimes whole days pinned to the couch, mulling over our history.

I could stare for hours at my posters of Elvis Costello, Johnny Cash, and Tom Waits: the Holy Trinity. Smoking dope taught me the joy/Zen of just sitting, or just lying down. Just staring. Just thinking. I excelled at mining old times to relive them, digest them, like an animal that has two stomachs and regurgitates food to eat things twice. I wasn't a hermit, my Isobel was coming over later for drinks.

Sullivan was the first person I met who actually loved Alberta. He never bitched like the rest of us in winter when it was minus thirty with a wind-chill factor of minus fifty during a two-week cold snap. He cross-country skied to work through the river valley trails. He made me paintings on bark. Most people dreamed of leaving Edmonton, for the coast or somewhere cosmopolitan like Montreal, but Sullivan saw the beauty in our frozen prairie city. He had a black Labrador always at his side, he canoed on the river, he made igloos in the winter with his friends.

He was woodsy. I was lipsticky. He basically introduced me to nature. And oof! what a discovery nature was: the wind, the stars, the air, the smells, the great outdoors. Sullivan showed me how to camp properly, how to start fires without matches, how to scope out the ideal site in the wilderness, how to cook over the open fire, how to smoke pot and sit naked on a mountainside just in time to catch alpine glow.

I loved the feeling of a breeze on my butt as I squatted to pee in the woods, the long grasses tickling my nose. Skinny dipping in mountain lakes. Drinking whisky around the fire. Cooking tomatoes in a can. I was a late bloomer in the nature revelations, but it was heady stuff to discover at twenty.

From what I can make out, some people marry their big heavies, some lose them and move on, and some are forever haunted by them. I wanted to have it again. That kind of love. But deep down, I was pretty convinced it would never be that big again, and so I had become the curator of a dusty, rundown love museum with the same damn permanent exhibition.

I used to blame my fractured relationship with Sullivan for causing my Nerve Problem. I thought he had broken through my pain threshold when he left me for good. Like my pain was somehow worse than the rest of the world's heart-break. I probably should never have read *Love in the Time of Cholera*. The guy in that story loves this girl from when they're teenagers until their eighties, even though the woman marries someone else and the guy lives in a brothel for twenty years. That book infected me with the notion that you could and maybe should love someone your whole life even if you weren't together, especially if you weren't together, and that equalled Pure, True Love.

That evening, Isobel said, "Let's get out of town . . . I want to put some miles between me and Finn." I, drunk on cheap red wine and a belly full of smoked oysters, proclaimed from my wobbly perch on top of the Cadillac couch: "I want to have Hawksley's babies! Let's go see his concert in Montreal. The gig on the mountain. We can meet . . . He can see with his own eyes how wonderful I am." "Go, sister, go," was Izzie's battle cry. We were Don Quixote and Sancho Panza.

I knew it was a good idea to hit the road. I'd been getting a little overly vigilant on checking the light switches and unplugging the appliances again. When that happened, I needed to squash the habit cold turkey. Get me away from the goddamn oven! It's definitely off. Off. And the couch; enough already. The more my left eye twitched, the more I knew running from the Problem was the answer because compulsiveness was often only the goofy precursor to something much harder to cope with.

The next day I had to pick up Rosimund from the mechanics—my 1972 pink Volkswagen Beetle was in for a tuneup (which was coincidentally perfect timing for our road-trip plan). I took the Number 7. The overwhelming silence of public transportation really gets to me sometimes, all those people, side by side, not talking. I automatically tried to sit as near to the exit as possible. I thought I was fine. At the next stop a big guy got on board and sat right beside me, practically on top of me. He didn't smell great. I tried not to think about how I couldn't just get off the bus whenever I wanted, and how I was going to the north side of town, which was pretty far away and I wouldn't be able to just run home. I tried to calm myself by imagining the drive home, having a smoke, and not having that horrendous muffler sounding like a dying buffalo. I worried about getting anxious, having an attack on the bus. That made me anxious, just having it in my mind, and once the thoughts started like that it was too late . . .

It was so unnatural the way people just sat there mutely, desperately avoiding eye contact.

The silence was strangling me.

The longer I dwelled on it, the more the pressure kept building.

Weirdly, I wanted to scream.

How crazy would that be? Maybe people would join in. Maybe not. Random screaming passenger. The pressure of stopping myself, restraining myself made me panicky.

I wasn't breathing right.

Oh no, here it comes again.

I was dizzy.

I was sweating.

I couldn't stop blinking, trying to hold it all together and somehow push back the wave of adrenalin flooding my veins. My heart was beating so horribly fast I thought surely I was going to break. This wasn't like my Dan Bern nerves. This was pure horror, like I was being buried alive, or was trapped in an elevator filling with water.

I had to get off the bus rightfuckingnow.

I rang the bell. I looked at the man at my side who was blocking my path to freedom. He was dozing, smelling pickled from the Old Stock beer poking out of his pocket and coming out of his pores.

"Excuse me, excuse me, sir?" He wasn't budging. I shook his arm. *What am I gonna do? I'm gonna shout! I'm gonna . . .* The bus swung to a stop. Guy was drooling. *Screw it, I gotta climb over him!*

I scrambled over the guy, half-straddling him, to get over him. Everyone looked my way. I got myself out of the bus, sweating and gasping, but relieved to be outside.

Except where was I?

Near some train tracks on 95th Street. *This was where the gangs that you read about in the newspaper live. Shit.*

It was still daylight, luckily. I ran up the busy street. Keys clenched between my fingers. Ready to stab someone if I had to. A small, old Chinese woman with a scarf covering her head looked at me suspiciously. I tried to give her a reassuring smile, to prove I wasn't an unhinged weird girl strung out on drugs. She shrugged. I passed Sinderella's strip joint, saw the photos of girls in ridiculous positions, all open-mouthed, like they were just begging to be filled up.

I ran the twelve blocks to the Fasto-Matic mechanics. The running was definitely helping exhaust my nervous energy.

I arrived, hot and sweaty and out of breath.

But calmer. Much calmer.

The mechanics were Italian twins, one shy, one talkative, both sweet. Funny Fellini farting scenes came to my mind, replacing the anxiety. I paid the bill, and they got Rosimund out of the shop. I drove home, relishing my independence. They had vacuumed it, shined the vinyl, and spritzed it with a pine smell. I opened the windows to air it out and turned on the radio, vowing never to take public transport again. I had a celebratory smoke.

When I got home, I went straight to bed and lay in fetal. I talked to myself as if I was my own doctor. "There's no need to jump to conclusions. We need to run some tests, to rule some stuff out, and maybe later we could do some electric shock therapy . . . But for right now my diagnosis is that you must be some kind of freaky weakling."

Later that evening when I woke up I put Hawksley on the stereo. I lay down on the couch, closed my eyes, and revelled in his soaring voice. As usual, I felt a wonderful warm wave of elation.

I unbuttoned my jeans. I imagined I was lying naked, basking in the sun. Hawksley sang about berry juice and wind on his soft places. I felt him singing to me, stroking my hair, loving my breasts, licking my skin. I arched and swayed and gyrated into a great sea of shivers. Airborne, in another dimension, until I crashed asleep.

When I awoke a little while later alone, miserable, with a dry mouth I reckoned it was time for whisky. Time to leave town too. Hitting the highway could be the answer. It was the one place I had never had the Problem. When I was on the road, when I was on holiday, my eyes didn't twitch, I didn't get the Attacks. Like a baby, I was lulled by the flow of tarmac and engine drone, wooed by yellow lines, white stripes, blue sky, and music on the deck.

I lit a cigarette and topped up my whisky.

My reserves broke down, and I did what I secretly wanted to do for months: I dusted off my calligraphy set and wax seal and finally wrote him a proper letter.

Hi Hawksley,
I can't hold it in any longer, my love and admiration for you. I've heard you sing in fifteen octaves, using your vocal chords one at a time or in unison like can-can dancers. I've been there when you

sang angel-style a cappella on a unicycle, played piano backwards and upside down and just for fun you played electric guitar with your house key. You take a concert hall, an outdoor street parade crowd, a bar audience, and make all the hairs on all the arms and backs of necks stand up and do the wave in a collective mass crowd shiver.

You are not just some kind of prophetic rockstar, tap-dancing, curly-haired boy wonder full of the right measure of masculinity and femininity. You are my Grateful Dead, which must make me a Hawksley Head, which sounds like I'm some kind of weirdo birdwatcher. Edmonton, Toronto, London, Antigonish, Tuktoyaktuk, Wayne, Hove, Waterloo—there's nowhere I won't go for you. I would consider parachuting if I had to (and I'm seriously terrified of that moment when they push you out of the airplane).

Me and my pal Isobel are going to drive the flattest, most boring roads in the world to come see you in Québec. I'll be in Montréal for your mountain gig, it'd be great if we could hook up . . .

I'll be wearing a red flower in my hair.

XOX Annie Jones

Before I could stop my brave tipsy self, I ran down the block and popped it in the old-fashioned mail because I knew he'd prefer it like that. I would have loved to send it by messenger pigeon if it wasn't so damn far for a bird to fly. I called Isobel to say let's go tomorrow.

She said oui.

"3,000 miles from satisfied . . ."
"Providence," Luann Kowalek

Day 1
Southeastern Alberta
400 klicks gone
+30 Celsius, late August
2 o'clock

Hawksley probably hadn't got my letter yet, and I didn't have time to wait around for his response. His concert was on in Montreal in seven days' time. So we left the next day as planned, barely prepared. As soon as we left those city limits, I got the familiar feeling that it was so utterly right to be leaving, it would have been wrong to stay.

Isobel said, "Allons Sud!" And my heart filled with joy at her oomph. Her oomph was one of the best things about her.

So south we went first of all, hoping for more sun and southern charms. We'd go east after Lethbridge. We knew it was shorter to cut through the States, but we didn't have our passports, and besides, it was cool to keep it Canadian. I was driving the first leg of the day and was trying not to fall into a trance from the hypnotizing pulse of the road. I'd decided to quit smoking on the road because as much as I loved my cigarettes they weren't helping the Problem. I'd taken long, luxurious drags off my last smoke early this morning. When I felt the smoke mingle with my adrenalin, I knew I was halfway there on the anxiety hellpath. The new me was on Chupa Chups lollipops instead, interchanged with watermelon-flavoured Jolly Ranchers. Isobel was smoking like a chimney, so I was matching her one for one.

Some time after Calgary, in an otherwise empty landscape void of anything but a flatlining horizon, any specks are a major event. Isobel was the first to notice a blob in the distance. As we got closer we could see it was a hitchhiker with a panama hat and a red bandana covering his nose and mouth and a cardboard sign with the message: PICK ME UP, I'M FRIENDLY.

We slowed down thinking it might be funny to have a hitchhiker. Plus the guy might have some food on him. The break from monotony got my heart pumping. I pulled Rosimund over to the verge, and Isobel got out to stretch her long legs. Shielding her eyes from the glare of sun, she sussed out the guy: "What the—how?!" I leaned farther over the passenger seat to look at the guy in case he was a wacko and she was in danger.

It was Finn! And Isobel was pissed.

"Get in the car, Finn. You're in big trouble. What are you doing out here, in the middle of nowhere—like roadkill?"

"Whoa, Isobel, take it easy! He's hitching, he could be going anywhere. Where are you going, Finn, and what's with the bandit bandana look?" I asked. It had become our habit over the years to work a good cop/bad cop routine with men.

"I, well, I kinda thought I might go to Winnipeg. I gotta protect my Celtic fair skin—" he said, untying his bandana and running his hand through his red corkscrew curls.

"Winnipeg, mon cul! Annie, he's following me!"

"Look, Iz, let's go get some doughnuts together and talk this out."

She made a sour noise, but she knew we couldn't very well leave him out in the middle of nowhere, so we got back in the car and drove for a while. The Tim Hortons I thought I'd seen in the distance turned out to be a mirage and was just a billboard advertising a Woody's World of Winnebagos lot off the highway. It was another fifty klicks to a service stop.

"I'm getting a heavy-duty canker sore. Ouch."

"That'd be from the ten thousand lollipops you've had already," Isobel I-told-you-so'd me.

"Excuse me, girls. Maybe we should stop on the side of the road? I gotta take a whiz—"

"Sorry, Finn. No can do—" Isobel said, passing him an empty juice bottle.

We drove on in mild discomfort because Finn had known we were going on this trip and it seemed like too massive a coincidence that he just happened to be on this patch of high-way today. The last time I had seen him was the day she ditched him and he'd vomited on his pants. He'd probably managed to get a glance at my map markings at the Sugar Bowl.

Isobel looked like a trapped exotic bird with her face pressed up against the passenger window. The windows were shut and there was no air-con. We alternated having the windows open and closed because a fresh breeze came with unbearably loud highway drone. I could see sweat beading up on Finn's forehead in the rear-view mirror. I was jealous that he had followed her all this way. I wished I inspired such devotion.

There was almost no traffic. I couldn't even remember the last car we came across. Eventually Finn broke the silence. "Alright already, okay, so I was jealous, I admit it. When I heard about you guys' trip, I wanted to go on a road trip too. I figured I could hitch to a ride to Winnipeg for the festival there. I had no idea you guys would be on this exact stretch of highway at this time."

"What are you going to do at the festival? Who are you going to see?" I asked.

"I thought I was on a roll after Bern, you know what I mean? And I thought I should keep up my infiltration of the rock journo world and try to get some interviews that I could write up for some weeklies."

We drove on in silence for another ten awkward minutes. I could feel Isobel trying to decide whether she should stop pouting or not. I liked him being with us. He had good energy. Plus he might know how to check the oil.

"Sullivan used to like this stretch of the highway," I said, trying to crack the silent bad vibes in the car.

"I think I should rig up some electrical device to shock you every time you casually mention his name in a conversation," Isobel said.

"What, like a cattle prod?"

"Seriously, it's worrying. Are you going to carry a torch for him for all of your twenties? He's just a guy. Maybe we should burn an effigy. You need some kind of purge. It's bagony for everyone," she said. (Bad agony, Isobel word fusion.)

Day 1 cont.
600-ish klicks
4 o'clock
Medicine Hat, Moose Jaw, Regina

Rosimund seemed to be doing well on the road. For an old banger rustbucket already carrying five hundred thousand klicks, she was heroic. I took an exit off the highway near Medicine Hat and drove down a dusty back road for about five kilometres until we were deep into nowhere land. Corn fields on the left, prairie grasses on the right, blue sky above. There were no cowboys, no farmers—just an old, greying barn that stooped in the field on the right like a prairie version of the Leaning Tower of Pisa.

"Oh, c'est triste!" Isobel said, gesturing at the barn, the general emptiness.

Telephone poles dotted the distance, carrying twenty-nine million people's conversations from Victoria to Antigonish through the quiet prairie. Sparrows and some kind of bruiser birds, accustomed to dry heat and wind, sat spread out on the wires in tribes of twos and threes. On a blue-sky summer day, this kind of landscape looked like freedom, but on a white winter day this same scene could make a person weep due to the wrist-slashing isolation of it all, or not; depending on your mood. I wondered when the pioneers and homesteaders came here, why did they stop? Why didn't they retreat or go farther west? What possible draw could this emptiness have? Had they bought land sight unseen and this is where it happened to be? How did they know they could survive minus fifty? It must have been summertime. Must have been a day like this one. Blue sky, yellow fields, and warm lover's breath air.

I parked the car beside yet another wheat field in this breadbasket of the country. We got out to stretch our legs and have a pee. We picnicked on red licorice and trail mix I'd grabbed from my kitchen cupboards along with some of Finn's homemade beef jerky. Finn spotted a long-tailed weasel in the grasses, telling us he knew it wasn't a gopher because of the brown tip of his tail. He'd been reading up on his prairie flora and fauna. He told us the names of all sorts of creatures we could hope to see like prairie skinks, white-footed mice, black-footed ferrets, coyotes, badgers, whitetail deer, northern leopard frogs. I especially wanted to see a prairie skink, what a rock 'n' roll name!

Driving through the flat bottom of Saskatchewan, we finally kicked into tranquil road-trip silence. It was liberating to realize we couldn't possibly talk the entire way to Montreal or there'd be no more saliva left. We were driving in the big abyss. The weird feeling returned that cities were something from our past.

A best-of Joni Mitchell tape played on the deck, Isobel drove, and Finn snoozed in the backseat. We were down by Moose Jaw. Endless prairie fields passed us by. I was so numbed by the sameness and flatness that I barely registered the bales of hay and dusty sideroad turnoffs. I wondered how much flatter the world could get. I thought Alberta was flat, but, Jesus, Saskatchewan was unbelievable. I dangled my toes out the passenger window into the blasting warm air.

It was still light out at ten o'clock when we decided to stop for the night to camp just outside Regina.

"'My father says that there is only one perfect view—the view of the sky straight over our heads,'" Finn loudly quoted *ARWAV* from his sleeping bag beside the car.

"'I expect your father has been reading Dante,'" I quoted back, yelling from inside the car. The warm air coming in the window smelled of ripe chokecherries. Iz and I decided to sleep reclining in our seats. I soon realized it was a big mistake for our necks and backs, all those restless sleepless body contortions in the chase for the perfect snoozing position.

Day 2
Regina–Winnipeg
1,046 km behind us
still 2,818 to get to Montreal!

We were so uncomfortable the next morning there was nothing to do but get started early, neck kinks and all. Got some gas station coffees and ice cream sandwiches to fuel us for the day ahead.

Seeing Regina from the highway, we thought it looked like a mini-Edmonton served up on a platter of extra flatness. It was still Isobel's turn at the wheel and my turn to choose the tunes. I had only recently lifted the Blue Rodeo ban because of all the Sullivan associations. Through past experiments I'd discovered if I listened to a song enough times it would stop reminding me of him. This worked with most bands we'd listened to together. Blue Rodeo, though, being his favourite, was tougher to crack because they, more than any band, had featured on our canoodling soundtrack. I knew it would probably be okay because they hadn't freaked me out back at the Folk Fest.

Normally I tried to keep a strict regime of letting my thoughts go Sully's way only once in a while; when I was safe on my Cadillac couch. I'd learned to let out the angst now and then to air it. See if it had composted any. But maybe if I went for broke, I could purge him somehow like Isobel said I needed to. Lulled by "5 Days in May" I gave way to thinking about him. The landscape, the open road, all this space was perfect for cud-chewing. When the tape played "Diamond Mine," followed by "Cynthia" and Jim and Greg crooned away, I surrendered to full-blown flashback mode, kind of like blowing your diet and eating a king-sized chocolate bar and then a block of cheddar cheese, a bag of nachos, and then Cappuccino Commotion ice cream—we've all had days like that.

Christmastime Three and a Half Years Ago
Mexico, December, +35 Celsius,
blue and cloudless = nuking sunbeams
Margaritas = icy cold and super fruity,
tequila arriba arriba

Under the zapping rays of Mexican noontime sun, Isobel snapped photo after photo as I struggled to write *I Love You, Sully* with my big toe in the sesame sand just above the surf. Behind us a band of eight sombrero-wearing, moustachioed mariachis played trumpets and guitarones and sang a song about a town called Guadalajara for a gaggle of Canadian tourists. Four times my *I Love You* message was erased by a returning wave. This was the spot on the beach where the sand was moist enough to have letters carved out in billboard size. I dragged my right foot and used my big toe like the tip of a giant ballpoint pen. When I finally got it right, Isobel snapped the photo just before the water came and erased it once more. We were on holiday in Puerto Vallarta for Christmas break, lapping up mangoes and camerones, stooging in hammocks under palm trees. Sullivan was at home in −30 Celsius, likely at the ice rink with his sister and her kids, being a good uncle. I hoped this sand note was going to make my coolest love message yet. I would frame it and give it to him for no special occasion.

He had hidden a card in my suitcase that I found when I unpacked the night before. The illustration on the front was of two penguins hugging.

Dear Annie,
I know we will be apart for a few days, really only six
sleeps, but I will be sending you telepathic kisses
and licks. Our bodies will be slip sliding soon.
Love, Sullivan.
six sleeps soon

We tried to outdo each other with love notes. I loved his gentle, loopy handwriting—curly like musical notes. He never used pens, always pencils. I guess he'd always had an erase clause.

It had been almost a year since we had collided in love bliss, and it had been some kind of sexual awakening for me. Sullivan and I had thundering sex in bathtubs, oceans, lakes, gas station cans, forest floors, mountainsides, trucks, motorcycles, hammocks, couches, chairs, and beds. We tried all those positions in that funny Indian book, even that outrageous one. My body was his to do with as he pleased; I had given it to him.

That first summer we were together, we were separated for a month because he got a gig working as a production assistant on a film set in Calgary. As many times a week as possible I would drive a hundred and fifty klicks south to the Glenn's diner in Red Deer on Gasoline Alley, the halfway point on the highway, and he would drive a hundred and fifty klicks north to meet me. We would go off the main road and park alongside a prairie field of spear grass and wild barley. I would climb into his truck and we would kiss and make each other come, and exchange mixed tapes and love letters and kiss some more. On nice days we'd roll around in wheat fields and have picnics. Sometimes we only had an hour to spend together, but we did the three-hour round trip regardless. The whole way back to town I would listen to his mixed tapes and indulge in flashbacks and desperately look forward to getting home to read his liner notes.

On holiday in late August, we discovered new hideaways all over Alberta. My favourite was Black Nugget Lake. It was our own private lake, only as big as a backyard pool and probably as deep, but it was sweet, isolated, and warm enough. After smoking a little reefer, we spent the afternoon naked on two water mattresses gently floating on the miniature lake. Encircled by bulrushes, we dozed in the sunshine like frogs basking on lily pads. Both evenings we camped there we spent in front of the fire, getting high, eating chocolate, sipping whisky, talking music, looking at the stars, hoping for northern lights. I was converted to the church of Sullivan and his way of doing things.

After I got home from Mexico I felt a subtle shift in him. I couldn't describe it to Isobel at the time; it was underground. He was still doing sweet things like leaving tulips in my apartment when I wasn't there, singing goofy love songs on my answering machine. But right from that first hug at our airport reunion—he'd come to give Isobel and me a ride— there was a new space between us even though our bodies were smashed up against each other. I tried to hug him harder, to wriggle closer, but we were as close as was possible. My stomach ached.

On the drive home I asked him: "How was your holiday?"

"It was great, you know, I did a lot of writing, some reading, saw some old tree-planting friends from out of town, played hockey with my nephews. I missed you. I wrote about ten pages in a journal . . . But how about you guys? Que pasa en Mexico?"

"Great, you know, mariachis, margaritas. Oh and Isobel had a fling with a rancher from Montana, Cowboy Bob," I said, nodding to Isobel, who was sandwiched in between us in the front of the truck. "You're not normally a journal writer, Sullivan, are you?" I asked.

"I needed to write some stuff down. You're always talking about your journaling and how it helps you think. I really want to think about moving. I've got to focus on my film stuff this year. I might have to head out east at some point. There's so much work in film being done out there . . ."

He was trying to work in TV and film production and learn as much as he could so he could make his own shorts one day when he rounded up enough coin. When he wasn't with me, he was working on film stuff; that and hockey. And it was hockey season all right. I stared at the blowing snow drifts on the black highway. The cold wind felt abusive after the lush moist warm Mexican air. It was the first I'd heard of him moving cities, and the way he never said *we* in his plans made me nervous. I wouldn't bring this up though, because I spent a lot of effort cultivating being the girlfriend who never laid the big heavy—it wasn't sexy.

But once the first suspicion was triggered, I couldn't stop fixating. I lost all power to divert my thoughts. Which old friends had come to visit? That girl who he shared a tent with platonically for six weeks that summer before we met? That old friend? The mysterious actress? In the past he had spoken fondly of her from time to time when his tree-planting stories came up, and I'd thought about Alicia but only seriously wondered on bad premenstrual days. But why had he suddenly taken up writing in a journal? It felt like he was taking out a press release that he had secrets.

Two weeks or so after being home from Mexico, on a weeknight, we were making dinner and I finally let myself relax. He was clearly devoted to me. He had gotten my favourite rice, was making his chicken à la Annie dish (chicken breast with ginger and pineapple), and he'd rented a foreign film I really liked that I had seen once on TV months ago and had mentioned in passing. He was so attentive, there was no reason to doubt his love; it was just me being neurotic.

We sat on the couch while the rice simmered on the stove and the chicken baked in the oven. He fired up an already rolled joint. Smoking dope amplified my appetite for everything, not just food. Music and sex were even more ecstatically enjoyable. Those days I was smoking a lot more pot but wasn't worried about it. Dope was another thing that he'd brought into my world. It wasn't like he corrupted me; before him, drinking and smoking were pretty much my favourite pastimes. With the added bonus of dope, every day was a celebration, a never-ending honeymoon. I took a big hoot and sank into the couch, revelling in the strange noises from the Asian-Arabic fusion music he had found on his travels before we met. The basmati smells fused with the music. I imagined us wearing ornamental silk outfits, sitting in one of those howdah things on top of an elephant making our way through carpet markets, passing men in tents sitting cross-legged, smoking hookahs. I wondered what Sullivan was conjuring.

The phone rang and jerked us out of our lazing. It was Jim calling. He was stuck in a Safeway parking lot on the north side of town. He needed a boost. He'd spent too long shopping and it was too cold for an old car not to be plugged in. He could have called a cab to come and give him a boost, but he knew Sullivan would do it because Sully was everybody's helper guy.

He left the house just as the music stopped. Alone, I could sense uneasiness creeping up on me. I couldn't concentrate on choosing more music to play. I flipped through his vinyl collection. I couldn't find the right tunes for my mood. I went to the bathroom and brushed my hair. I dabbed on some peppermint lip balm and put more eyeliner on my glazed eyes. My hands weren't so steady from the dope. I smudged it three times in a row and had to take a break so I wouldn't get overly compulsive about it.

Dope paranoia had kicked in. I thought about Sullivan saying two weeks ago how he'd kept a journal. If I just read it, I could put my doubts away for real, once and for all. Peace of mind might be worth a minor sleazy transgression. I stared hard at myself in the mirror. I wiped off the eyeliner; it wasn't helping. I knew the doubt would only get uglier and infect everything. But I thought of my own journal and how if anyone read it I would be gutted.

I went back to the couch and sat down. I lit a cigarette and contemplated the sleaze factor. I was no longer stoned; I had scared myself straight. Sullivan would be gone for at least forty minutes. The chicken was cooking in the oven, the basmati was simmering. Reading his journal would be for a greater good—safeguarding the purity of our love. But I didn't want to. It was wrong. My stomach hurt.

But maybe he actually wanted me to read it, why else mention it? I went around in a loop.

The phone rang. Sullivan said, "Listen, honey, it shouldn't

take too long, we've got the car started finally. He's out of gas too, so I gotta go get some, but I should be back by nine. Can you check on the chicken?"

"No worries."

I got up off the couch and went to his bedroom. I scanned the room. I saw his navy blue backpack lying on the floor. I was drawn to it. Everything felt pre-scripted. I could anticipate my own melodrama unfolding as I just followed along the obvious path.

I reached my hand into the backpack and pulled out a binder, a mixed tape, a little baggie of dope, a mottled banana, and a recycled paper notebook with a purple cover. I peeked inside and saw several pages of pencilled words.

It was so easy to find, must've been fated that I read it. I paused and took a breath.

December 26
Annie left today for Mexico. I was sad. But kinda glad. Could use a little time alone. Didn't tell her that, she's a great girl. Had a good going away party with a fantastic hut. I don't know, guess sometimes I worry she just loves me too much. I love her a lot too, I do . . . But it almost feels like she wants my soul, she wants to climb right in. I don't know. We connect well though . . . Am excited about seeing the old crew from Avola. Tree planting that summer was crazy. Have to admit it'll be nice to see Alicia again too. I've been thinking about her a lot lately, since she sent that letter I guess—

I paused and reread the name *Alicia*. My brain felt foggy.
I reread the word. It started with an *A*, but no matter how
many times my eyes shuffled the letters they never spelled
Annie. I closed the journal.
My guts ached. I exhaled.

December 27
Christmas was fun. Annie called. She's having a
blast in Mexico with Isobel, drinking margaritas,
having mariachis play for them.
    Heading over to see Alicia now at her cousin's
place.

December 30
Holy Shit!!!
    I gotta write this stuff down. My head hurts.
I went over to Alicia's on Thursday. Her cousin
had left for Calgary for a couple of days, so it
was just her there with an apartment to herself.
It was so easy to be with her. She looked great.
She's got this gorgeous long red hair and sexy,
slightly bucked front teeth and those different
coloured eyes of hers . . . She made a pot of
peach tea. We smoked a little cone. She played
me Tom Waits' new album. We took a shower.

I stomped on my emotional brakes and stared hard at
this line and reread it like it was my biggest enemy and I
could outwit it by scrutinizing it to death. *Then we took a
shower. We took a shower, we, shower, took. We took a shower.
We. WE?* I wondered if there was any possible way he meant

they took one after another. I jumbled the word order in my mind, trying to translate all possible meanings of an obvious phrase. I could feel adrenalin gaining momentum in my veins, bypassing the roadblock of denial I was trying to cauterize myself with.

It just happened.

I knew what had happened. I felt a sick thrill. The excitement of something important happening. Like an accident scene. My own personal accident scene. I kept reading, to get the facts, like a vicarious witness; I read on as my heart fell to the floor, leaving me hollow inside.

> We soaped each other and made love in the shower with the steam all around us. Like water animals. I love Alicia. It was seriously hot being with her like that.
>
> Had to leave her to pick up little Jack at his hockey practice for his mom, but as soon as I dropped him off, I went back to her house. Rolled around all night. I was in a fog. A good fog for three whole days. She's got this hard to describe angel-like quality. I don't know what it is. Think I'll always love her. No matter what.
>
> Said goodbye this morning. She was headed back to Ontario, back to her boyfriend I guess. And Annie comes back in two days. Don't know what I'm gonna tell her. Probably nothing. I mean, I can't explain it, I just, I don't know. It's that old thing, what she doesn't know won't hurt her. I hope . . .

I examined the little doodle sketch he had done of Alicia. She looked like a Venus de fucking Milo with long curly princess hair. I put the journal back in the bag by his desk. Sitting on the desk was a framed picture of me and him in Jasper. Smiling ear to ear, both of us. Blue sky above and noble Mount Edith Cavell shouldering us in the distance.

I walked to the kitchen on wobbly legs. My eyes blurred and twitched. I remembered to stop holding my breath. I gripped the counter, determined to stay standing. I poured myself two-thirds of a glass of vodka and then topped it up with orange juice. I could almost laugh at the melodrama but not quite. I just knew I somehow had to stop myself from falling to the bottom of a well.

I turned the TV on, volume low, got the phone and called Isobel, and before she could say hello, I said calmly: "Listen, Isobel, don't worry, I'm fine. I am fine. I just need to stay on the phone with you and not cry. Okay. I don't want to cry. That's the thing: not to cry."

"What's wrong, sweetheart? Do you want me to come over?"

"No, no. I'm not at home. I can't tell you right now. Sullivan will be here any minute. It's just really important that I don't cry. Talk to me. I just need you to talk to me. Tell me anything. Tell me about your day."

"Let's see . . . I was dog sitting today for Frank, t'sais. So I went to Whyte Avenue with Cona and walked around. She tried to mount some poor woman on her lunch break. Got her paws all over her silk trench coat. Very bad. Though what she was doing wearing a silk trench coat on a cold-ass January day I don't know!"

As she talked, I thought about the water sex thing and how I had assumed it was something Sullivan and I had invented. "So then, Cona took an obnoxiously large dump right in front of

Army & Navy and I didn't have any plastic bags, so I seriously had to hightail down an alley and run a few blocks so I wouldn't get chased by a cop on a mountain bike and get a fine!"

I heard the kitchen back door close, and Sullivan saying, "Shit. Shit. Shit." Then there was a cacophonic clanging of pots. The basmati must have been annihilated. The chicken probably nuked as well. For the first time I noticed the burnt smell and smoke filling the living room.

"Look, Isobel, I gotta go. I'll talk to you later."

"Sweetie, I'll come see you tomorrow. It's gonna be okay, ya?"

"See ya."

Sullivan walked into the living room where he found me smoking a cigarette and drinking my orange juice, oblivious to the kitchen crisis. I looked up from Brian Dennehy on TV and smiled. "Mind if we go to my house and pick up something to eat on the way there?"

Sullivan looked at me and must have seen something like quiet hysteria in my unblinking eyes. I could tell my smile was twisted. He didn't ask about why I had let the food get wrecked, or why I wanted to go home. "Sure," he said.

He must have known I knew, that I read it. Or he would've asked why I let everything burn.

Outside it was pitch-black except for the white snowbanks and the lit road ahead of us. We drove past the neon sign by the funeral parlour that always had the temperature listed. Minus 26 in big digital orange letters. The truck's vinyl seats had rigor mortis. But I wasn't tensed up from the cold. I was sitting comfortably as we drove across town, crossing the frozen river on the High Level Bridge. I chatted aimlessly, oddly determined not to let any of the horror out. "Brian Dennehy, you know he's not a bad actor, but he's always playing these overworked cops . . . except for that movie about his belly, you know in *The Belly of an Architect*, he was awesome in that. But that's it, I mean, otherwise it's these bullshit movies of the week. I wonder if he minds . . . It's like . . ."

Sullivan kept taking his eyes off the snowy road; I could feel him looking at me, no doubt trying to gauge the damage. I knew he was anxious; he was scratching his chin. He knew I knew. Had to. But he was keeping a lid on it for some reason. I could hear him scratching, couldn't stop himself. I took a peek at his profile. He looked seedy to me then, like a squirming rat. But he had such beautiful eyelashes. I jerked forward as the car swerved on the black ice under the snow. The truck was shimmying up the street. I didn't care. Sullivan gripped the wheel, his arms rigid. I wasn't wearing my seatbelt.

All that was important to me was that I hold it together until after dinner. I was divvying up the future in increments: dinner, home, eat, reveal, break up. Only once I was on my home turf could I act.

When he got to a snow-cleared street he fiddled with the radio tuner until he got the university station. It was angry music hour. He went to turn it off.

"No, leave it on, please."

It was jolting, loud, screeching heavy metal full of primal screams and lots of Satan references. I'd never been a metal fan, but I found it suited me—it was animal enough for my mood.

We went through a drive-through A&W. He got a bacon double cheeseburger and fries, I got a cheeseburger and a Root Beer. "You sure you don't want some kind of sundae? Like the kind with broken cookies that you like?" he yelled to me over the music.

"No, thanks. I'm FINE." I lit my third cigarette of the truck ride off the end of my second. Chain-smoking was my only solace. I pledged myself to cigarettes for the rest of my life. They were my mercy. And now heavy metal too, apparently. I could relate to the headbanging urge. Nihilism was the clear way forward.

I didn't know how to look at him. I was so used to looking at him with love, with lust, with curiosity. What now? Loathing? It was all disbelief and confusion because, somehow, somehow I could still feel his love. It just didn't make sense. I focused on the sweetgrass hanging from his rear-view mirror.

We pulled up in front of my five-storey brick walk-up apartment building on 105th Street, one of Edmonton's only truly steep hills. Once inside, I put Peter Gabriel on the stereo, turned on the string of Christmas chili pepper lights. Together we arranged the food on the coffee table. I pulled out my duty-free vodka from Mexico and made us both a cocktail.

There was no way I could eat my meal. Smoking and drinking were possible, but not eating, no way. The burger was repulsive. The bun looked like processed paper pulp, the meat was plasticky, the condiments gelatinous and leering. I let it sit there untouched, wasted. I ate one soggy fry and regretted it. He slowly, stupidly chewed on his burger. I could see that each mouthful was harder to chew. Mayonnaise seeped out of the corner of his mouth. I smiled tightly at him. I felt that stale fry sit in my stomach by itself, squirming.

I thought I was bluffing successfully but wasn't sure anymore why this was important. Now all I wanted was for him to eat all of his food. It was important to me that he had his dinner, I didn't know why.

Finally he was done. "Aren't you going to finish yours? Or start it even?" We both knew I wasn't going to, but he mustn't have been able to stop himself asking and going through the motions. I didn't say anything. He cleared the table and went to the kitchen. I listened to him scrape the plates, my burger made a thud as it hit the bottom of the garbage bag. He gulped down a glass of water and the leaky tap dripped.

When he finally came back in the room and sat down opposite me, I looked at him and said firmly, "Let me just start by saying: I know."

"What?"

The tap dripped.

"I'm fully aware that I shouldn't have, but I did. I read it."

"I read it," I said a bit louder.

It was amazing how instant his reaction was. He clamped his hand over his mouth, gagging, and then got up and ran to the bathroom. I could hear him vomiting. It felt appropriate somehow, that deep retching noise, the appropriate soundtrack for this hell. It took him a while, and I went over and over the thing that stumped me, that I couldn't wrap my head around. I lit a cigarette and topped up my drink with more vodka. We weren't some stodgy couple with no romance left—we were still honeymooning. My guts ached. My insides felt like they'd been mugged and beaten to a tender pile of bleeding pulp.

Finally, he came out of the bathroom and sat down. After a few minutes of silence, he cried. I watched the candle on the table. I didn't say anything. He was howling. I wasn't. He leaned his head against the wall and then pulled away so he could bang it, trying to head-butt some redemption.

"Stop it. Please don't."

"I don't know what to say. I'm sorry. I'm so sorry—" He banged his head against the wall again in a horrible refrain.

I was glad to see a tangible sign of his regret, but I didn't like to see him hurt himself. And also I was angry, he was stealing my stupid thunder. This was, after all, my primetime victim slot. I could feel a horrible sarcasm rise up over the ashes of my broken soul. It beckoned me to feel the perverse kind of power that comes with being the hurt. I knew the hurter would have to go to Herculean extremes to win forgiveness. Was he entitled any pain of his own? I guess if he hadn't any, he'd just be an asshole.

Any of my other boyfriends would have been out the door over this: Bob, Joe, Clayton. But this was Sullivan, my wonderful Sullivan. That night of revelation, I drank more vodka, he smoked and cried. I don't know why, but we went to bed that night and fucked like strangers. I couldn't believe he'd done this with someone else. Me, who put chili in his cocoa, lavender on his pillow, and peppermint cream on his feet.

After sex, I got up off him and saw blood running down my thighs.

My period. I went to the bathroom and washed myself off. Then I went to the living room and grabbed my cigarettes before climbing into the bath in the dark and letting the water fill around me.

After soaking for ages, I let myself pee in the water. I was about to get up when Sullivan called from the bedroom, "Can I get into the bath?"

"Sure," I said and got out.

We were diseased after Alicia. There was no cure. Like my friend Randy rudely put it: "You know, you try to get over these things, but there's no getting around the fact that when you go to bed that other girl's pussy is going to be there in the bed with you both. And when you wake up in the morning, guess what . . . her pussy still going to be there! And like they say: three's a crowd, baby."

We'd almost crossed Saskatchewan and Blue Rodeo were long finished their B side so I hit stop on the tape deck and sat up. I would never be able to figure out why it had gone that way with Sullivan, why I hadn't been enough for him. But now that I'd lost him, I had nothing else to lose. The little guy in my heart bouncing on a trampoline—hoping, jumping, leaping, trying—had been in a hammock ever since it all ended, taking one long timeout until now.

"C'mon, Isobel, you should take a break, let me drive, I swear I won't pull over for any more hitchhikers." It was then that Finn yelled, "Hills! Girls, girls, we're headed for hills."

"It's a mirage, Finski, une mirage. It's time to camp for the night, on est tous un peu zinzin."

It was dark by the time we parked in a field somewhere near the Manitoba border who knows where. We had a trusty pack of wet wipes for cleaning ourselves, a bottle of water, and some caramel popcorn and more delicious beef jerky for nourishment. We were practically pioneers. Finn slept diagonally in the car and we slept on my trusty air mattress, just beside the car. It was hot enough to sleep without the tent and not too many mosquitoes. I spotted my lucky Orion above.

"so fuck you and your untouchable face"
"Untouchable Face," Ani DiFranco

Kiss of Life

Day 3
1,567 klicks
800-ish to Ontario

The big green highway sign said MANITOBA 50KM in white letters. My lips were sore from shelling too many salty Spitz sunflower seeds. I was twitching for a cigarette. Licorice wasn't really cutting it. The road ahead was blurry with heat haze. It looked like we'd soon be driving through a giant vacuum bubble that might transport us up up and away to another dimension. If I could choose, I wouldn't have minded going back to Jane Austen's time, when a kiss was a major big deal, when love brewed slowly over singular moments exchanged in ballrooms and on the moors. Good conversations over infinite cups of tea discussing species of flowers in the garden. Wit and decency reigned in Austen stories. And I detected some good lust too, even though she never quite described it explicitly. All those brooding, swaggering horsey men though . . . Maybe I needed to move to England. Henry James said the English were the most romantic of all people. And you can really see that, with guys like Morrissey and D.H. Lawrence and E.M. Forster and Oscar Wilde, or actually wasn't he Irish, and Morrissey too—maybe it's the Irish I need. At least there were actual people over there, unlike here in this prairie void.

Finn slapped his thighs. "Okay, that's it then. Before I head home I think we need to check someone out. And then, poof, I'll be gone and it'll be your road trip again."

I could see by the way she inhaled that Isobel was running out of patience with him. Earlier, I'd heard them having a just-friends discussion when I was pumping gas. She'd told him that it was our road trip and even though he was a great sport it was time for him to go. She squashed his remaining hope by saying she would never date him again, and that he had to move on. She invented a Québécois boyfriend who she said she was going to hook up with in Montreal: François Saucisse.

"Who wants to bring a sandwich to the buffet?" she said to me in the gas station can. We both knew the percentage of hot men in Quebec was astronomical. I was fond of Finn. It was mean to relegate him to the sandwich category after all he'd been through with us.

"If you guys come with me to the Winnipeg festival, there's this singer we can see. Apparently she's mind-blowing. Life-changing. Remember, Dan Bern told me she's the most dynamic live performer since James Brown," Finn said.

"Who's that?" I asked.

"Ani DiFranco."

"Is she Italian?"

"Maybe, I don't know, but I've been talking to people, and she's supposed to be unbelievable! Don't you remember Dan mentioning her during the interview, toward the end?"

Finn knew he could always woo Isobel and me with stories of some musician-god that we just had to see. He had witnessed and even participated in our ritual of getting new music and having listening sessions together. We had strict rules: Lie on the floor. Eyes Closed. No Speaking. Careful Listening to All Lyrics. Discuss and Replay to Catch Nuances. Lots of music was grower music, the kind you had to play over and over until it clicked. Sometimes it was that music you ended up liking the most. The kind you struggled to like at first. Other music was obviously just loin-dazzling, mind-whirling, kneecap-buckling on first listen. What we specialized in, what really got us going though, was pathos. Little notes that struck big portentous moods. Over-the-top Janis Joplin–type scratching voices, screaming with hunger. Yearning and moaning. Lying around listening carefully to music was what we did when we weren't at the cinema, or the bookstore. We'd been doing it since we were fifteen. Maybe that's why I fainted; it was such a habit to be lying down, to better hear the music.

Lots of wannabe participants had failed over the years, had been banned from our music-appreciation club over breaking the No Speaking rule. Not a lot of people were as devout as us, or as precious about it, I guess. And many people didn't like being shushed aggressively during our holy rituals. Part of our weirdness probably came from our parents: my dad was a Dylan fanatic and had every album, every bootleg recording, every interview, article, and book in print, and Isobel's mom was big into all the crooners, but especially Tony Bennett. We weren't churchgoing families; we were raised with this version of sacred.

Isobel glanced at me then in the rear-view mirror to ensure we were on the same page about going to the Winnipeg Folk Fest. I cherished our non-verbal way of communicating, but I saw Finn feeling excluded. I wriggled in my seat.

"Oui, on y va!" Isobel said. "We still have four days before Annie needs to be on that mountain."

"Great, I think it'll be wild! I should be able to find some Edmontonians to hitch home with there too." He would've sounded almost serene if he wasn't speaking so rapidly. Maybe he'd given up the idea that Isobel was going to fall in love with him again. He had literally gone the distance, almost sixteen hundred kilometres, to find out what he needed to know— that she had never been in love with him.

But he was acting with a kind of grace and generosity of spirit that made me want to make her love him, force her somehow. I loved that he organized adventures, even hijacking a rock star for us. I don't know why Isobel couldn't fall for him. He wasn't mysterious enough, I guess. He was an open book. A book with lots of great pages, though.

When I tried to psychoanalyze her, I never got very far. She was immune to men on some level I couldn't begin to relate to. I saw her detachment as the strength and independence that I was lacking rather than emotional incompetence.

She was driving because my foot was asleep and there was a strange nervousness in my stomach. I could feel the end of summer and the season turning in the melancholic winds of late August. When I was little I used to think of the last two weeks of August before school starting as two straight weeks of Sundays with the Monday doom looming over your head.

We mostly bypassed the small towns of southern Manitoba with Isobel reading and relishing the French-named places from our trusty roadmap: Portage la Prairie, St. Boniface, Dauphin. Manitoba was the country's heartland; even colder than Alberta in the winter and definitely hotter in the summer. I was starting to get sick of the drive, it was feeling like the

Wednesday morning of the workweek. Our collective bums were numb and our joints were aching from sitting in the same position for hours.

It was the driest time of year. I was parched, and we were out of water and there was no gas station in sight. The sky was baking blue. I imagined the farmers, in their plaid shirts and GWG overalls, sitting on their verandas thinking about going out into the field to do one big collective rain dance.

We listened to Neil Young because it was Neil Young's province not just Winnie-the-Pooh's. We tried to imagine Winnipeg bars back in the day having Joni Mitchell and Neil gigging together. No wonder people made great art here, there was nothing else to do, nothing to clutter their young imaginations, just big sky. I watched the fields passing by. More prairie, endless prairie.

Finn stuck his head out the window like a dog—looking like happiness personified. Finn was the dog that yapped at everyone's heels, doing tricks, rolling around, playing dead— anything to win affection. From the backseat I could see Isobel look at him sunning himself out the window. She smiled; half amused, half irritated.

Eventually we found the festival, forty kilometres north of Winnipeg. It was in beautiful Bird's Hill Provincial Park. The whole layout had a great mellow vibe despite there being upwards of sixty thousand attendees. And the usual scene was there. Hippies, dippies, old-timers, Hacky-Sack-playing teenagers, toddlers, earnest folkies, patchouli girls, tie-dyed natty dreads, and hempy people. We roamed the grounds and sat down on the grass in the beer garden. Finn went off to get us beers and mini-doughnuts. I was happy to be lying still with the sun on my face with my best friend at my side. Lying on our backs always led to truth sessions—being horizontal meant being intense.

"Are you sure you couldn't fall for Finn?" I had to ask.

"Well, honestly, j'ai essayé. And I do wish I could, seriously. I don't know why I can't . . . I guess I'm like some kind of self-contained unit." She looked sad confessing this to me. It occurred to me then for the first time that her inability to love Finn wasn't just another non-event in her long line of contenders contending. It was a failing. Not unlike my own failings. I went too far; she couldn't go deep enough.

"But feel free to go for him, Annie. You know you and Finn could make a good pair!" Isobel added with a cheeky smile.

"What? Don't be ridiculous! No way. But . . . he is great, you know," I said.

The mainstage show was coming on in ten minutes so we tried to get closer, but the field was filling up quickly. A man in drag was on stage doing a shtick about the discomfort of porta-potties: how when you go into one later in the day and it's at capacity and you've had a few beers, you somehow gotta try to hold your purse, plug your nose, and negotiate taking a whiz—it's tough to hover in those conditions! And you're truly screwed if you had the god-forbidden hot sauce with the green onion cakes and your intestines are in a hurry to evacuate.

There was something different about this crowd. It took me a few moments to clue in that it was because it was mostly women and girls making up the whole area. They were mobbing the stage. Dan Bern must have been on to something with this Ani Diwhatever.

Isobel wasn't comfortable with lots of women around. Was she threatened? God knows why, she was a Queen Bee. But I was pretty much her only female friend. I could see her bristling at other good-looking women. Women were looking one another up and down all right, but in a women-are-beautiful way, and don't they wear nice things. Like raccoons drawn to sparkly objects. In this crowd I think she was the only one doing accounting; everyone else was smiling. I didn't care that we were road-trip grubby.

It was hot. Hotter than Alberta and more humid. Mosquito count was not too high. They must have sprayed. Bumblebees whizzed over the crowd of femaleness. I glanced over at Finn; he looked pretty happy. Lovelies of all descriptions surrounded him. It was a short-haired, long-haired, curly-haired, Sinead O'Connor shaved-headed, bead-wearing crowd of women smiling in anticipation. Only a handful of men joined the throng. Most of the other guys stood back, watching from afar.

I had never been around this many women before in one place. It was a different energy than at a male performer's gig: Isobel elbowed me to get my attention and nodded toward two women arm in arm, shaved heads, and only wearing black PVC bras underneath their denim overalls. They had big black stompy boots and a kind of girl warrior chic I had never seen before.

"Psst, Finn . . . psst . . . is this some kind of lesbian event?" Isobel asked.

"Lesbian event, what do you mean?" Finn repeated.

"Shh," came from someone behind. I turned to look and it was a ten-year-old girl with braids and an orange T-shirt with the words QUESTION AUTHORITY written on it. She was standing beside an older girl who looked like her sister whose T-shirt said READ CHOMSKY.

A roar surged through the crowd. There was no one on stage yet but thunderous clapping, ground-stomping, and cat-calling came bursting from the audience. Whooping went on for minutes, building a tidal wave of suspense. The excitement was contagious. I was filled with anticipation for I didn't know what.

And then—a small woman walked on stage.

She was five-foot two-ish, like me. She was wearing a motorcyclist's black leather vest, low, hip-riding jeans, and clunky workman's boots. She had muscular arms and a tattooed collarbone. Ani DiFranco was wearing an Alvarez Yairi WY1, Finn told us. It looked like it might overpower her, but she had a good grip on it, curled in the curve of her breast. She had big, full lips, super-white teeth, a shaved head, wide sparkling blue eyes, a nose ring, and hairy armpits. She was gorgeous!

She started to tune her Alvarez guitar, and the crowd quieted down, anxious to hear her. She spoke up: "You know, people say I'm an angry girl, but uh . . ." She giggled. "I just got a few things on my mind is all." Her laugh was charming. I could see that she had black electrical tape on her fingers and I wondered what for. Then she hit the guitar with this crazy Spaghetti Western fury, crackling through her galloping chords. It wasn't a matter of her warming up or the crowd warming up to her. Everyone was hooked straight up and straight in. I could understand the tape now, it was so she wouldn't get raw, bloody fingers from playing so crazily hard; like she was trying to break the speed of sound. She played like thunder to her adoring crowd of shaved-headed young followers, hippie girls, suburban preppies, mothers, sisters, and grandmas. Girls, girls, and more girls danced in the front rows, danced so hard the sun-baked ground rose in a dust cloud among us all.

She sang anthems. I looked around; all the girls knew all the words and were singing their hearts out:

> I am not a pretty girl
> that is not what I do
> I ain't no damsel in distress
> and I don't need to be rescued
> so put me down punk
> wouldn't you prefer a maiden fair
> isn't there a kitten
> stuck up a tree somewhere

There was no leather-trousered male in sight on stage, but I was falling in big-time heart-throbbing love. A new kind of hero worship had hit me.

She had breakup songs. She had revolution songs. She had fuck-you songs and fuck-me songs. She had the gift of the gab. I had never seen anything like it before. She was no earnest folkie. She was no ridiculous Madonna serving up her sex on a platter, pretending it was original. She was fresh and raw and playful and flirtatious with her shit-disturbing politics, her vulnerable love songs, and her way of playing guitar that sounded like she was twanging all our collective nerves and veins and ligaments. It was visceral and incandescent. I could see fire and mountains and lashing rain and gyrating bodies and tranquil seas, trembling desires, lusty encounters, and brave acts. It was all there, coming out of her little body and mighty fingers. Ever since she started playing, I'd had a tingling feeling at the base of my skull. A creeping feeling of well-being. It was new, tingling instead of twitching. I was connecting, part of something, and proud. I wasn't even conscious that I had lost Isobel and Finn. Mouth agape, I just let it all pour inside me through every orifice and pore. It felt like watching a natural disaster, from a safe distance.

Between rocking songs, she played some jazzy improv music and just started talking while jamming, like Van Morrison does sometimes: "You know, there's a lot of bullshit out there in the world for girls to wade through . . . I was in a clothes store the other day and I was shocked to discover the latest fashion crime: size zero. Have you heard of this? I'm serious . . . it's for real. I mean, what the crap is that? No really, what the hell is that? I was just trying to buy like a gaunch or something . . ."

"Whooooooooooooo," roared the crowd, egging her on. She stopped talking and lost herself and put all of us in a trance with the wacked acid-jazz medley she played on electric guitar.

"Since when are women built to be a size zero? And is that the point, that as women we should strive to do nothing but spend our time starving ourselves just so we can be a *zero*? You wouldn't see a guy buying a pair of size zero pants, now wouldya? I mean, God . . . But anyways . . . we got way more important shit to do . . . like world domination! Ha! . . . I'm no zero, are you guys zeroes?"

"Noooooooooooooo . . . woo . . . woo . . . woo . . . rrrrrrrrrrrr rr," whistled the crowd.

"I don't want to preach at y'all, that stuff just pisses me

off and I gotta get it off my chest!" She laughed again and snorted in an endearing donkeylike way, hamming it up. She must have been the class clown. She finished tuning, and a few chords into her next song, the crowd went nuts. "Blood in the Boardroom," it was called. The audience was euphoric.

> Sitting in the boardroom,
> the I'm-so-bored-room,
> listening to the suits talk about their world
> . . . I wonder can these boys smell me bleeding
>   thru my underwear.
> They can make straight lines out of almost
>   anything . . .
> I can make life. I can make breath!

I was in the throes of the crowd, celebrating bloody underwear! Lifted by the group's oozing exuberance, I was transfixed. I had been moved; just like all these women beside me had been at some point or another when they first heard this woman. My body was a fusilli noodle, at one with the crowd and tunes, swaying and bending, contorting and springing. Ani DiFranco sang in the sun for an hour, driving us crazy with her percussive finger-plucking. People threw roses and incense, T-shirts and books and lipstick and food and panties on the stage. We danced through her twenty-song set. The music went straight to my hips. I was deep in the heart of this crazed crowd. We danced so hard, we were dirty and dusty and smiling big. Her final rock encore was so intense, the dancing so enormous, the sky clapped and a sun-shower came down on us and washed the dust off our faces and made some mud for our feet to play with and splash up our legs.

The crowd wouldn't let her leave the stage, so she took a swig of water, sat down, and put a tam-tam between her legs. She sang Prince's "When Doves Cry" a cappella. Just her ragged voice and the brooding drum. It was hair-raising and beautiful like a swim at dawn. I was listening so acutely, almost gulping in all those lovely sounds she made. I saw her biceps beating the tam-tam and I understood how important it was to be fully alive, fully engaged with life. It was like sunlight, after years of candlelight. I'd been too much of a night owl, spent too much time indoors with the curtains drawn.

I had been rapturously inspired before, many times, but I'd never had a female hero before. I made a run for the record store tent. I had to restrain myself from pushing people out of my way to get to her stack of CDs and tapes. She had several albums, but I could only afford two of them. I chose her first one and her most recent release on cassette because then we could play them in the car. I read some of her liner notes while I waited to pay. She was only in her twenties. She had her own record label: Righteous Babe Records. Behind me there were dozens of young girls trying to get their hands on her music.

I made my way back through the crowds, heading to where we had been sitting before the show, figuring Isobel and Finn would know to go there. I was buzzing with excitement, dying to share the experience with them. So excited, I could barely breathe. What a rush to see a woman do it like that—get up there and kick serious musical ass.

Plowing my way through the crowds I wasn't really concentrating on where I was going and I walked smack into a girl. I actually head-butted her by accident. We both rubbed our foreheads and looked at each other.

"Sorry, wow, I'm really sorry about that," I said.

She had long romantic red hair and peaches-and-cream skin with freckles. I felt a cloud of foreboding when I looked at her one hazel eye and the other green one. I scrutinized her face, wondering what the likelihood was that this could be the same girl, the same buck-toothed *free spirit* Sullivan had written about.

She laughed and rubbed her forehead again. "You're sure in a hurry for a person at a folk fest, is there someone you gotta see?" Her laugh was scratchy and sexy.

Was this really her? I hope she's not an Ani fan too.

Cowboy hat, a mini-skirt. She's just like I dreamt her to be. Except in my nightmares she was larger than life and I was a Lilliputian.

I must have fainted. Again.

Am I sleeping? It's warm and I'm tired. Oh, oh . . . what is that? Am I being kissed? Jesus, what's going on? That feels weird. My nose is itchy . . . I tried to shake my head back into consciousness, my eyes were heavy and I felt a mouth on me again. A dry, unfamiliar mouth, smothering me. It was breathing into me. Then it pulled away.

The next time I opened my eyes just in time to see her mouth coming toward me. She was plugging my nose too. There was a tent of red hair cascading around my face. She tasted like something tart, something . . . iced tea.

I jerked up when I understood finally what was happening. The she-devil was giving me mouth-to-mouth artificial respiration.

"Hey, are you okay? You just fainted. You passed right out. And I didn't think you were breathing . . . I think we gotta take you to the medi-tent."

"No, no, I'm fine, I'm sure it's just the sun, the beer, the dope, the music, you know . . ."

"Well . . . shit. Are you breathing fine?"

"Ya, thanks for that, Alicia," I said, still confused.

Her eyes opened wide. "That's not my—"

I took off running, through the crowds, hoping she wouldn't follow me. I rubbed my mouth with the back of my hand, trying to rub off her bizarre kiss. I felt stung, and slapped. After I was sure I was lost in the crowd again, I stopped for a rest breath and went to hide behind a Moroccan food tent. Gasping. An old man came back to get some more supplies for his kiosk. He looked at me and said, "You shouldn't take drugs, you know, it's very bad for young girls." Then he wagged his finger at me, like an elementary school principal. He grabbed a water bottle from his cooler and gave it to me. I drank it all in one long gulp, grateful once again for the sweetness of strangers.

I shifted my canvas arm bag from one shoulder to the other. I remembered the Ani DiFranco tapes and pulled them out. I sat down in the shade of a tree. I looked at the crowds around me, making sure I was anonymous again, with no demons in sight. I pulled out Ani's song lyrics. My eyes were bubbling over with tears.

Untouchable Face
tell you the truth I prefer
the worst of you
too bad you had to have a better half

she's not really my type
but I think you two are forever
and I hate to say it but
you're perfect together

so fuck you
and your untouchable face
and fuck you
for existing in the first place
and who am I
that I should be vying for your touch
and who am I
I bet you can't even tell me that much

. . . y'know, I don't look forward
to seeing you again
you'll look like a photograph of yourself
taken from far far away
and I won't know what to do
and I won't know what to say
except fuck you

The words weren't 100 per cent relevant, but they were pretty damn close. I remembered her singing them. I badly needed to hear her singing them again. Once we were back in the car, I could play them over and over. I would put the she-devil out of my mind, forever, she was just some hippie girl like thousands of others, a girl just like me. And maybe it wasn't even her. It didn't matter anymore anyway, his infidelity. I was a woman who was moving on. I had new music to lead the way.

I found Finn and Isobel sharing a beer. "Holy shit! That was incredible! I mean, wow. She rocked so hard I can't believe . . . she's made of fireandwaterandsmoke and passion, hallelujah . . . !!!"

"Calm down, ma bichette," Isobel said.

"Isn't she awesome!" Finn agreed.

"Pas mal," Isobel said.

"Not bad? She's a revolutionary, a radical. A hero!" I gulped.

"I don't know . . ." Isobel said.

"What's not to know? She rocked!" I was ending our conversation right there. I didn't want to sully my high with irritation. Isobel's blaséness disturbed me. She had to have been affected. Surely. What was the problem? Finn took his last sip of beer, then stood up.

"Well, see you, girls. Thanks for the ride. Thanks for the laughs. I saw Joe over there, and he said I can camp here for the weekend and go home with him."

I looked over at Isobel pleadingly. Now that the time had come, I was sad to see Finn go. I felt it in my stomach. He had become part of our unit. He brought us to Ani. But she was unflinching. I hugged him for what felt like a long time. "See you soon, Finn. Thanks for everything."

"No worries, Annie. I hope Hawksley gets a chance to experience you and fall passionately in love like he should." He looked at Isobel and she said, "Salut. Arrivederci, Adios, hombre." She was trying to be breezy but was falling flat. Finn reached out and tucked her hair behind her ear. He nodded at me and walked away.

"Well, I guess we should go to the can and then get back on the highway. We can listen to the Ani tapes! Unless, you feel like sticking around?" I asked, trying to detect any signs of doubt about Finn in her eyes.

"No, let's go quickly. I don't want to keep bumping into him after this."

Back on the gravel parking lot, I took the wheel. Isobel dozed off almost as soon as I started the engine. I was amazed she could be sleepy after that gig made me so high. I put in one of Ani's tapes with the volume on low. Whenever my mind drifted toward that girl, I steered it back to Ani. I drove away singing along to the little bits I'd picked up and tried to imagine what it would be like to be her. To be a travelling minstrel. Taking the Greyhound bus from city to city. Sleeping in late, staying up late, having adventures, living on the road, having big diner breakfasts, loving and leaving. Writing beautiful poetry in cafés. Wowing crowds across the continent. I wanted that lifestyle so badly it made my mouth go dry.

I replayed the concert in my mind, relishing again the high. All the girls there at the show seemed to be veterans, singing along, knowing all the words. They were part of a world I knew little about. The kind of people I saw at health food stores who read *Ms.* magazine and boycotted Nike. I had been missing out. It felt like someone had taken my perspective with her bare hands and adjusted it with a major screeching crank so I could see better. It felt big. Isobel was snoring.

At the next gas station, while Isobel snoozed in the car I went to the payphone and collect-called my dad.

"Hi, Pops."

"Hi, sweetheart, how are you? Where are you, by the way?"

"Isobel and I are on a road trip. Sorry I didn't let you know before."

"Where are you headed?"

"To a gig in Montreal."

"That's a long way for a gig! Did they give you time off work?"

"No problem, Pops. Listen, did I ever faint as a child?"

"Are you okay, Annie? Have you been passing out?"

"Just a few times lately. No big deal, I just wanted to know if you remember me doing this."

"Actually, when you were really little, I mean quite small, up to my knees, I'm not sure what age that was, you used to hold your breath until you passed out. It used to scare the hell out of us. It was either a matter of will, being stubborn over something, like Brussels sprouts, or it was a nervous thing, like during scary movies."

"I totally forgot about that."

"Well, you were pretty young. Are you okay? You're not taking drugs, are you?"

"Dad!"

"So when am I going to see you? We could go to the movies, or book hunting—you could come stay for the weekend."

"Okay, Dad, when I get back from Quebec. See ya."

"Take care."

I felt a little melancholy after that call. I loved my parents, I don't know why I didn't make the effort more to see them. Since they'd split up, only a few years ago, everything was so strained.

But the holding-breath thing resonated. A memory came back of my older brother making fun, counting down as my four-year-old self puffed out my cheeks, ready to hold my breath for Canada over I don't know what tantrum. "You're going blue, no PURPLE! TEN, TWELVE . . ." He missed a number and I opened my mouth to tell him so. He won.

Isobel often commented on my sighs. I forgot to breathe sometimes, so I had to catch up with huge big gasps.

I vowed to breathe better.

"Holy shit!"

"What's going on?" said Isobel, waking up.

"There's rocks and hills, trees and bumps and water. It's not flat. Not flat! Are we dreaming?"

"Incroyable!"

"It's weird though, isn't it . . . You can't see for miles anymore. I kinda miss the horizon."

Isobel looked at the map. "This must be the Canadian Shield!"

"I've heard of that." We drove on, mouths open, taking it all in. All the variations of landscape we'd been deprived of having grown up as prairie girls. I liked it, despite having the sensation of being under a smaller sky than I was used to, I liked the hills, the valleys, the rock, the views of higgledy-piggledy bogs and lakes. It seemed more alive, more engaged than the big empty.

By nighttime, we'd forgotten all about the flatness that had been with us for days on end and in fact for our whole lives. We were in a whole new province, a big one: Ontario. We found a beautiful campground near Kenora along the shores of the Lakes of the Woods and unpacked the car. It was so great to be near water and trees with the dusty prairies long behind us. Under the Mexican blanket in the backseat was

Finn's guitar. I was amazed he'd left it. Around the campfire later that evening, Isobel admitted that it was kind of sad without him and his floppy eagerness. She said he was like a golden retriever. I went to the car barefoot, crunching on pine needles, sap, and dirt. I got his guitar, thinking it would somehow invoke him. We could prop it up on the picnic bench and pretend he was there. Isobel unzipped it from its case. It had a big black mark on its blond wood.

It was a scribble. *To Annie—Hey Nice Name! kisses, Ani DiFranco.* Finn had gotten his guitar signed to give to me. I was beyond touched. It was undoubtedly the biggest gift I had ever received. My own guitar! It had never occurred to me that it was something I could have.

I'm not sure how Isobel felt though.

She just sort of looked at it and looked at me. I couldn't read her face in the dark with the slim light from the crescent moon above and the fire crackling on its last red embers.

"You are a china shop and I am a bull
You are good food and I am full"
"You Had Time," Ani DiFranco

Day 4
2,360 km behind us
Kenora, Ontario, to as far as we could get

Rosimund was starting to feel like an old beast at twenty-five years of age with thousands more kilometres of asphalt behind her. Bangers were like the senior citizens of the highway; you had to respect them and revere them for their mileage. Each day when I climbed on board I said a small prayer to St. Christopher, the patron saint of road trips and rustbuckets. Tom Waits had that funky song that went: "Hang on, St. Christopher," something something something, that had been growling in my head for several klicks.

Throughout the morning I couldn't help periodically checking the rear-view mirror. I was half expecting to see Finn again, this time maybe lying on the highway, weeping, after being dumped by Isobel yet again. Getting dumped by the same person in multiple provinces gave Finn a tragic trans Canadian epic character. The car felt massive without him in it, though. He and his voice had commanded a lot of room.

"Do you think he'll be okay?" I asked.

"Who . . . Finn? Of course he'll be fine, he's a grown-up!

Besides, if he can follow me to Manitoba uninvited, he can de-invite himself back home."

"That's pretty harsh."

"Tough love, baby, tough love. Guys are born heartbreakers. If I hadn't busted him up a little, he might never understand the value of a girl's heart. C'est pas evident, mais I'm clearly doing the female race a favour."

"That's a bit arrogant, don't ya think? Besides, don't kid yourself, Finn isn't like the others. He didn't need your guerrilla training."

"Musicians, especially, need to be tamed," Isobel argued.

"He's not really a musician and you know it. He's only learning. You just don't date anyone you like too much, that way you're in control. And that's cheating, you're never in danger . . ."

"The stupide thing is, Annie, guys actually like being treated this way. I'd cut him loose already, and he was back for more. It's bizarre but simple: girls like jerks and guys like bitches. Or if you prefer, some of us are cats, some of us are dogs. I'm a cat." She lit a cigarette and reclined her seat. "You like him, Annie, because he's a male version of you in some ways. That's why I like him too." She took another drag and exhaled vigorously. She often punctuated her dialogue with cigarettes—sending smoke signals to end conversations.

We drove across northern Ontario heading toward Thunder Bay in silence, listening to tunes and watching the lines get swallowed up by the car. Isobel seemed to want to stop at every single gas station can. It seemed she'd developed a toilet obsession. Meanwhile, I was focusing on the music to stay sane. I calculated that most albums would take us just over one hundred kilometres. We had played REM for three hundred kilometres. Going though their backlist. Crooning to "Everybody Hurts." Thrilled with "Losing My Religion." Loving "Ain't Got No Cigarettes" except feeling a little schmuckish because I did have cigarettes and was puffing away again.

There was no keeping track of the amount of dead bugs on the windscreen, but we kept count of the roadkill on the tarmac. So far, we had counted sixteen gophers, thirteen unidentifiable smashed and bloodied feather piles, obviously former birds, a few domestic cats, and lots of rubber.

As we drove past bloody gopher number seventeen, I wondered if it was possible that a girl could have experienced one night that could just skewer her off into mankillerdom. A bad enough night. A bad enough man. That was too simplistic, it couldn't actually have been just that night or just that man that made Isobel the way she was with men now. Her own father had been no beacon of male evolution; he had left her mother for his two mistresses, ending up in therapy for being a pigamist (one of Isobel's word fusions), and apparently even his therapist fell for him. Too much disappointment in the male species had given Isobel the armour that I coveted. I was a turtle without a shell, while Isobel acted like she was all shell.

I chose to blame Hubert. Hubert was her Sullivan. For both of us there was a discernible before and after. It was definitely AH (After Hubert) when her heartbreaking career started: Jimmy, Johnny, Bill, Donald, Justin, Sebastian, two Davids, three Daves, etc., like bloody gophers strewn across her past.

Five songs and two cigarettes later, I could see her in my peripheral vision deliberately jutting out her lower lip so that smoke came streaming out perfectly positioned right under her nostrils. She was trying to learn how to French inhale like we saw someone do in a pop video the other day. I was nostalgic for all things smoky. We had first started fooling around with smoking at fifteen with our headbanger friend Florence. Florence and her unicornesque feathered hairdo. She tried to teach us how to blow smoke rings in the air while we skipped math class.

By dusk time Rosimund was struggling. Something felt kind of off. Nonsensically I focused on the axle. Oh God, not the axle, I thought, not that. Not that I had any real understanding of what an axle might do. Isobel was snoozing obliviously until the bumps woke her up. She had become more despondent as the day wore on and unusually quiet. The more we drove, the worse the car noise got. It started to feel like we were the Flintstones, in a dinosaurmobile, as each spin of the wheel wahlumped. It was mysterious and sinister. I missed Finn.

Eventually it dawned on me with forehead-slapping-reality: we had a flat tire!

I knew I didn't know how to change a tire and Isobel definitely didn't get that in her Hubert training package. I pulled over to the shoulder. I had learned from wrecking Sullivan's bicycle that you can seriously damage a vehicle by driving it with a flat tire. I could hear him saying, "Jesus Christ, what is it with you and flat tires, already?" Shaking his head but still smiling.

The inside car light had probably died sometime in the 1970s, and we had no flashlight. Luckily Isobel had her '50s vintage bronze Zippo lighter. We looked at the map. There was a place called Wawa about three klicks away. Wawa. What kind of name was that? We stood beside the car with our thumbs out ready to hitch a ride on that quiet stretch of highway. My mother's voice rang through my mind with her various mantras for me: "Stay away from the bushes, strange men hang out in them. Never hitchhike, only murderers pick up hitchhikers. Druggies hitchhike too. There's more to life than the mattress. Men don't buy cows when they get the milk for free . . ." The aphorisms of my youth have stayed with me all these years, but nothing about flat tires had stuck.

"Annie, I can't do it anymore, this rough-and-tumble life-style of ours. I need some goddamned luxury. Maintenant!"

No cars came and the darkness was spooking us out. You never knew what maniacs were lurking. Though you had to wonder if maniacs wouldn't want to be closer to amenities? We hoofed it up the black highway. I think it was almost eleven o'clock, and the last of the late summer light had faded for the night. I thought I could see a light on the horizon. A hotel where we could splash out and spend the night. The neon gave me hope.

"I'm ashamed I don't know how to change a tire. We're grown women. It's the 1990s. How can this be, we're so back-wards? I don't even want to tell them at the hotel," I said.

"Look, relax, dammit. We're urban people, not mechanics. We'll just pretend we didn't have a flashlight, and it was too dark to do it. I'll sweet-talk the front-desk guy," she said.

I was hungering for some scapegoating, I was bloodthirsty, given our current state of lameness and my unresolved anger about Finn and probably even some angst over seeing that two-colour-eyed hussy woman. "For some reason, I've been thinking about Hubert," I said.

She looked at me, wide-eyed. "That's odd that you should mention him."

"Why?"

"I do not want to talk about it now. How far is this Wawa town?" She was blowing air up to her fringe to keep her hair out of her eyes, a sure sign of exasperation.

"On the map it looked pretty near, I don't know . . ." If I strained my eyes it almost looked like the neon blob in the distance was a castle.

We kept walking. I thought about the Bistro, glad that we were now in a new era of our lives. Before Sullivan and pre-Isobel-mankilling, just after graduating from high school, she and I used to go to Bistro Praha after going to the Princess to see foreign films where women with pouty lips smoked long cigarettes and men listened to opera in the bathtub. Stranded in our rodeo-riding, big-trucking, mullet-wearing northern wasteland, we lusted for the cultural orgy of Europe. Luckily there were some real live Europeans in our midst.

Hubert, the thirty-six-year-old waiter at the Bistro, had the same name as the cheap pink champagne that we liked to drink. They both had travelled all the way from Czechoslovakia. He was suave in that brooding Eastern European way. Maybe if we hadn't seen *The Unbearable Lightness of Being* over fifteen times, he wouldn't have seemed so sexy and appealing to Isobel. He had thick black hair with swirls of silver. He wore a stiffly starched designer white shirt with French cuffs and silver cuff links. He had a flashy watch and Italian shoes. Immaculate, he was more movie star than waiter, and at thirty-six he was way too grown up for eighteen-year-old Isobel—or so I thought.

Bistro Praha was famous in Edmonton. Through the restaurant grapevine, I had heard that Wilhelm, the owner, paid his waiters a real salary instead of the normal minimum wage that most waiters earn. It meant that the staff weren't overly concerned about tips, which made them complacent and even picky about who they felt like serving. Anyone who looked too vulgar, or like a hockey fan rather than a theatre patron, was told at the door: "Dis place is not for you." Young women, though, were pretty much always welcome. When difficult customers aggravated his waiters, Wilhelm was famous for confronting them: "Are you being rude to my waiter?" He was well liked around town for his gregariousness and for his notorious belching. His trademark party piece was to guzzle champagne straight from the bottle; all those bubbles speeding down his throat caused some historic burping. On special nights I had seen him sabre the neck of the champagne bottle with his special blade that he said he'd robbed from a Soviet soldier in Prague, circa 1967.

People also went to the Bistro to hear the wisdoms offered by Shahi, the Hindu dishwasher who boasted he was one hundred and two years old. He claimed he stopped eating long ago and sustained himself on Holy Brown Cows (kahlua and milk). He liked to come out from the kitchen on slower nights and pronounce a few mantras. One night he walked by our table and said, "Girls, you must approach all matters slowly, calmly, and peacefully." I wish to this day, I'd properly absorbed that maxim. Mindfulness was not one of my fortes. Nor Isobel's. I never saw how she managed to think Hubert was charming.

"Vat do you vant?" was his standard opener. He had a boxer's puffy lips. He didn't smile. He stared at you with an I-am-so-sophisticated-and-European-and-you-are-clearly-uncultured-Albertan-hicks look. Isobel, as usual, was less intimidated than I. She liked his bossiness and gave it right back at him. "Pink champagne, two glasses—and quickly!"

"Could I please have some ice water?" I would ask while Isobel pouted provocatively like femmes do particularly well in French movies. I knew that Hubert had a personal policy of not serving water. I always asked, though, as a matter of principle.

"Oo, I feel a frisson in the air, I think he's starting to notice me!" Isobel whispered one night when he walked away from our table. I think this was the fourth time he'd served us.

I leaned forward to reply, "That's not a frisson, that's a goddamn draft from the front door being open."

The Bistro was downtown on a quasi-European boulevard in a row of terraced cafés. It had mahogany furniture and antique lamps. One wall was covered in a wallpapered-mural, a pastoral scene. I thought it was kind of cheesy and so, trying to make light conversation the first time I met Hubert, I blurted, "You know, I think this wallpaper has gotta go!" Then I smiled at him.

"This is a scene from a very special place in the countryside of Czechoslovakia, outside of Praha. It means a lot to Czechs who come here, people who have been exiled from their homeland."

"Oh . . . I . . ."

He turned away, to focus on Isobel. "Zo, tell me again, vat you think about Milan Kundera?"

"Well he's a pretty smart guy, obviously, but, what do you think?"

"You do realize he is Czech?"

"Of course," Isobel said, flaring her nostrils.

"I think, you couldn't possibly have an understanding of

such things at your age. He is a genius, light, heavy, light and heavy, you understand?"

"Well, I . . ."

"More champagne?"

"Yes, please."

He snapped his fingers, and his brother Josef came over; they spoke in Czech. Josef smirked and went to get another bottle and a flute for Hubert to join in. He opened the bottle expertly, easing the cork out slowly so it let out an elegant quiet pop, the bubbles frothing like a diamond waterfall.

My toes were now aching from this long Ontario highway walk, and my backpack was making permanent indentations in my shoulder. Isobel somehow walked elegantly, her high-heel sandals clickety-clacking, sashaying up the road.

Eventually I had stopped going with Isobel to the Bistro. Hubert got on my nerves too much, and I had developed a bad habit of snorting over his pomposity. The snorting got so regular, Isobel finally had said to me, "Frankly, Annie, you sound like a farm animal, and it's cramping my style." So she started going in to the Bistro by herself with Milan Kundera novels tucked under her arm. Usually she described these evenings in detail on the phone when she got home. She said she normally read and drank until he was finished serving tables and then he sat down with her and taught her what he felt she needed to know. Once he took her for dinner on the north side of town. He stared at her aggressive way of clutching the knife and fork in her fists and plunging into the food. He looked her in the eyes. "Don't."

"Excuse me?"

"Don't." He gestured to her iron-fisted cutlery grip. "Look at me, look at my hands. You see der is no need to use your whole hand to hold dem. Just use your thumb and dis finger here," he said, pointing to his index finger.

"What an asshole! Unbeelievable. Who does he think he is, trying to dampen your gusto?" I said when she told me the story. I still remember the feeling of my blood boiling.

But Isobel kept going back. His lessons included outfit consultations: "Vear red, very good for your complexion. Vear short black skirts, very good for your legs. Vear less eye makeup and less perfume." He edited her with almost free rein. He got her some fake glasses, gave her a silk scarf. He told her to cut her hair in a Juliette Binoche blunt. He said it was unattractive to snort when she laughed. She started to look thirty instead of twenty. It was like she'd gone to Ye Olde Hubert's Boot Camp for Nymphs.

Bored by the walking, Isobel finally piped up.

"Look, I know you disapproved of Hubert, but it was an invaluable education. And he wasn't so bad, you never saw his nice side, and you're hung up on that whole water thing. You know in Europe, nobody drinks tap water. It's just not done."

"Whatever. The guy was a major ass." I said, annoyed by vestiges of his pretentious imprint still on her psyche. But that was nothing compared to his disturbing sex ed curriculum. She had never told me the full details of the Table 12 night, but she had alluded to it in passing. Cryptic mumblings during our sad song sessions.

"What happened with him, Isobel, really?"

"You want the minute-by-minute account of how it finally happened?" Isobel asked as we slogged our way to the neon that was looking more like a constellation from eons ago than somewhere we could stay for the night.

"Yes," I said, rolling my shoulders and trying to readjust my heaving backpack.

"Okay then . . . If you're sure . . ."

"Yes."

"I met him on a Sunday night, after closing time, around nine o'clock. It was strange, going into the empty restaurant with only one lamp lit. He made a point of locking the door behind me. Something that sounded like 'Napoleon's March' was playing. Remember Table 12, the one by the back of the Bistro, near the wallpaper? He had an ice bucket with an open bottle of bubbly with a white scarf around its neck, two champagne flutes, and a plate of chocolate-dipped strawberries. I sat down. He looked at me meaningfully and coughed. It was my signal to stop slouching, so I did. He offered me a strawberry. I had one. It was ripe.

"So then he goes, 'You like that? Den you can have another one, but first . . .' and he unzipped his fly and said . . . you're not going to believe this . . . he said one word: 'Strip!'"

"Oh God no, tell me he wasn't re-enacting the scene when Tomas seduces Teresa?"

"Ya, so I played dumb. 'What?' I said.

"'Strip.'

"'Uh, okay.' I started pulling off my clothes.

"'Slowly. And look at me.'

"'You want everything off?'

"'Of course. Here, have another strawberry.'

"I chewed the strawberry and pulled off my skirt. I was wearing a garter belt like Sabine. I undid the two snaps on each leg. The stockings rolled to my ankles. When I was done, he said: 'Take me in your hand. Your right hand.'

"'Take you? Take you where?' But then I clued in as he looked down at me knowingly. I was sitting, he was standing. I went for a swig of champagne and thought, What the hell. I reached into his fly and grabbed his cock, trying to pull it out of the flap of his silk boxers. I wrestled it out, bending it and twisting it at an angle.

"'Be careful. Iz not an ee-lastic band.'

"I got it out, scraping it a bit against the metal of his zipper. Once it was out, I went to pull down his trousers.

"'No.'

"'But—'

"'Much sexier like this. Take me again.'

"So I picked it up, right, and started to try to whack him off. I started out like a freight train kinda, you know what I mean? Chug a chugga chug . . . a chug.

"He put his hand on mine and guided me. 'Think three-quarter time,' he said.

"I had to suppress a giggle attack over the oom pah pah thing. After a couple of bars, he put another strawberry in my mouth. I was a little freaked out, but focused, you know. I wanted to get this right. This was way better training than *Cosmopolitan* magazine. Let's face it, it's not like that guy I lost my virginity to was illuminating, with his two minutes."

I could tell by the look of glee on Isobel's face that she was proud of her war story: it was when she got her stripes.

"'Now stand up. Turn around,' he told me. He grabbed my hips, bent me over at the waist on Table 12. I was eye level with the salt and pepper shakers. He put himself in to me. I wasn't quite ready.

"He thrust.

"He waited.

"He thrust.

"He paused.

"He thrust.

"My lower back was cramping up a bit. He was breathing heavily. Every time he withdrew, I exhaled. And then he thrust again and this time the salt and pepper fell over!

"'Don't vorry, I had a vasectomy. Have another strawberry.'

"He walked away. I heard running water and the sound of him washing his hands as I stood up and straightened myself. I was sore and sticky.

"'Vee have to go, the cleaners will be coming soon. Come see me this week, ve'll talk about your performance. You did well.'

"I got dressed and left. He didn't call me a taxi. I walked up Jasper Avenue. It was 10:00 PM and Edmonton looked like a ghost town. It hurt a bit to walk, and I felt foolish in my high heels. I imagined I knew what it felt like to be a hooker. A glamorous movie hooker, though. On 105th Street, some rednecks driving one of those cheese-ball Trans-Ams with customized monster-sized tires rolled down a window to yell, 'Hey, wanna fuck?'

"I went home and drew a bath. I finally felt like une vraie femme."

I remember the key parts of the Isobel-Hubert saga that followed the big night because I was there. After the Salt and Pepper evening, later that week, Isobel and I were out for a late-night cheese fondue at Café Select. Inspired by its Parisian namesake, it had the best atmosphere of any Edmonton restaurant and was open until well into the wee hours of the morning. You could show up after a gig at two in the morning and still have a croque monsieur or crème caramel and a Kir Royale, our all-time favourite drink. We loved it there, especially the lighting—the main room was lit entirely by candles in little glasses on each table. So romantically dark. And they accepted our student-issue MasterCards!

We skewered little pieces of French bread and swirled them around in the Swiss cheese and kirsch fondue while Billie Holiday sang soulfully. All the good-looking waiters with their great hair and silver jewellery wore black and carried trays high on their fingertips as they manoeuvred like Latin dancers between the tightly packed tables and chairs.

That night I watched the hostess with the dog collar and nose-ring greeting two new customers at the door. They were an elegant couple; he was wearing a trench coat and she had cropped blond short hair and red lipstick. The hostess led them past us. Isobel looked up just in time to see Hubert with his hand cradling the woman's back. He passed inches away from our table, looked right at us, right into Isobel's eyes, and said nothing. Smirked a seedy smirk. They sat a few tables away. We could hear them speaking Czech.

Clutching a fondue skewer, Isobel looked like she wasn't breathing. "Look at that," she hissed.

"What?"

"He's wearing a wedding ring! He never wore it at Bistro Praha, the slimy bastard, jerkoff asshole jackass fucker!"

Hubert sat there, out of earshot, looking blasé and unconcerned. He and the woman were drinking champagne, the real stuff, Veuve Clicquot with the orange label. After the waiter took their food order, his wife got up to go to the bathroom.

He elegantly tossed his fork on the floor. When he got up to retrieve it, he walked over to Isobel: "Come see me on Tuesday." She was too stunned to respond. She looked down at the bill on the table, paid it, and rushed us out of the restaurant. "Isobel, you're not going to go see him, are you?" I asked.

"Vat did you expect? Don't be so naive. How old are you, twelve?" Hubert said on Tuesday.

He made her feel so stupid she gave him a blowjob to prove she was no child.

I felt raindrops on my forehead. Such a novelty added to our plight, almost making it an adventure. Isobel pulled out her pack of smokes and gave us each one. It kept raining. I loved it. So romantic to smoke in the rain, who could resist? Not me. We didn't get so much of it back in Alberta. A lot of snow but not a lot of rain.

As the sky continued to spit lovingly down on us, we puffed away in silence, contemplating the past. For weeks she had kept going back to Bistro Praha. I tried to get her to give him up, but apparently he was addictive. He unwittingly gave her an arsenal of tricks to please a man; twenty ways to make a man follow you around town. It was mainly an attitude thing. From him, she learned the art of aloof. The more blasé he was, the more she craved him; like a good student she incorporated aloof into her makeup. Isobel was now, as a matter of ingrained habit, always elusive. It did seem to come rather naturally to her, though.

Since Hubert, she said she'd rather that boyfriends left her apartment immediately after sex. He had eroded her *A Room with a View* idealism into hard-hearted realism. She was now more La Femme Nikita than Lucy Honeychurch.

From what I could make out, her dismissal served to fuel men's desire. Like Finn, for example—he seemed to want to keep running into the brick wall. I knew the lure of powerlessness. I had tried so hard to inspire Sullivan back, long after his feelings for me had atrophied, long after I knew it was hopeless and I was shaming myself. I deliberately stayed in a purgatory of yearning just for the sweet masochistic sake of it.

The hotel was in sight when Isobel let out a long sigh and said: "But you're not going to believe the really, really, really, really, really messed up thing about this all, Annie. I've got to tell you something else: the sequel.

"We had a reunion for old time's sake, about six weeks ago. It could be the worst, stupidest most *con* thing I ever did. Long-term repercussions . . ."

"What are you talking about?" Dark scenarios clouded my mind. I imagined his wife found out, her heart got broken. Divorce. Traumatized kids, the works. Or no, did she catch something from him? No condom usage, that was awful. "Fuuuuuck!" I said.

"I haven't had my period in four weeks. It's true I can be irregular, but this is definitely out of the ordinary irregularness. What am I going to do? My parents will kill me. I'm only twenty-four, I've got no income. I'm Catholic. And besides that, I'm not ready for a child. I want to travel. I need to pursue decadence and a career, and champagne consumption would have to go way way down. Chriss . . . Osti de Tabernak!" She always swore in Québécois when she was really worried.

"Whoa, Iz. Calm down. We don't have the facts here.

First of all, you're not really Catholic, c'mon now. What we need to do is get you to a doctor and get you a test, you've got to know for sure. Didn't he have a vasectomy?"

"I thought so, but I don't think it's the kind of thing a girl can check. There are no visible vasectomy signs, are there, like strange wrinkles? Fuck fuck fuck. Listen, I have a pregnancy test in my purse that I've been carrying around for two weeks. I keep going to the toilet but not doing it. I can't actually bear it . . . finding out that I'm pregnant . . ."

"But you can't not know. You've got to know. You have to make decisions. It might be Finn's."

"Do the math, Annie," Isobel said. We'd both failed Math 30 in high shool. It was hard to see her expression in the dark.

"Do you have any symptoms? Morning sickness. Sore boobs?"

"I'm not sure, I might have just wound myself up so much that I'm convinced I'm queasy. And I've been drinking and smoking and worried sick about fetal alcohol syndrome. And, Jesus, how would I support a baby? I am a baby. My credit cards are all full . . . maybe I could get some department store cards . . ."

"Don't talk crazy, Isobel, you don't know yet. You're very irregular." Four weeks late, what are the chances? Man oh man.

"Remember when I had sex with that sleazy guy by accident. And how I freaked right out and thought I had to get an AIDS test? That was the scariest day of my life, waiting in the waiting room. You came with me that day and waited with me. And we survived that whole scene. We're going to go through this together!"

If Isobel was pregnant, our whole lives would change. Could we still chase Hawksley? My mind wandered selfish terrain. If she was pregnant, might that possibly put her into a less sexy category and might I be elevated? Horrible, selfish, bad Annie thoughts. I reprimanded myself.

Just then a car passed us before we could even think to stick out our thumbs for a ride. Luckily the orange neon sign for Chateau WaWa loomed on the horizon.

"All right, I'll do it. I'll take the test," said Isobel.

The hotel had a vacancy. It was no palace, no charming pensione, but it was warm and friendly. And it offered forty-buck rooms—good for budget warriors. It was the kind of place where tired and lonely sales reps stay after a day on the road covering their rural territories, schlepping dental floss products or microbrewery beer or whatever. The lounge was open until 2:00 AM. In the lobby, there was a flip-chart advertising KaRa-O-Ke and Hot Buffalo Chicken Wings (twenty-five cents each)! Isobel looked twitchy under the fluorescent lighting. I saw sweat above her upper lip. I wasn't used to her being the nervous one. Now that she had finally let out her secret, the anxiety was contagious. I took care of the credit card stuff while she carried our bags up to the room. I felt sick thinking, PREGNANT, she's pregnant, she's definitely pregnant. She shouldn't be carrying suitcases, she's pregnant!

We settled ourselves into the room. It had thin, beige carpet, a small double bed with a golden chenille bedspread, beige curtains, and some bad nature art: a squirrel eating an acorn with a helpful heading that said, NEVER PUT OFF TIL TOMORROW WHAT YOU CAN DO TODAY. Isobel surveyed the mini-bar for supplies. I cranked up the radio for some acceptable tunes. Pulled the end table drawer open and the Gideon was there like it always was. Opened the blinds to see what kind of view we had: a parking lot with two long-haul trucks, big rigs with the engines left running.

Leading up to the test, we didn't speak. Isobel drank four glasses of water, and we waited until she needed to pee. I thought about baby prams and car seats, baby hats and shoes. The logistics of it all. I racked my movie brain, running through any relevant and helpful baby plots. *Three Men and a Baby* was the only thing I could think of, and Tom Selleck was hardly helpful to us now. I imagined a baby Hubert and a feeling of horror washed over me. He was a chubby baby wearing a lime green tennis shirt with a sweater tied around his neck, the way only Europeans or serious preppies do. His baby hairdo was Brylcreemed like his father's and he looked askance at me, pursing his puffy baby lips. "Of course jou can't have vater!"

"What?" Isobel asked.

"What do you mean, what?"

"Why are you in spasm?"

"It's nothing, I just got a chill, that's all. Are you ready?"

"Guess so."

We pulled out the instructions. Isobel lit a cigarette for courage. Pretty straightforward stuff. She was to pee on the stick. Red meant no and blue meant yes.

"This is like diving into a cold ocean. Just gotta plunge, Iz, plunge."

"Technically, it isn't plunging, Annie. I gotta splash on it."

"You can do it. I'm right here."

I climbed into the bathtub for moral support. She shook as she pulled down her underwear to sit on the porcelain. A cigarette hung out of her mouth. I handed her the white plastic strip.

"Go for it. It's gonna be fine . . . You'll see . . . We'll deal with it . . ."

"Geronimo," she said as she peed a big stream, deluging the stick.

"Jesus, it didn't say piss like Niagara Falls . . . but that oughta do it! Give it to me."

She gave me the stick, and I sat in the bath holding it, staring at it, willing it to be red. Isobel got up, went over to the sink, splashed water on her face, and then started tweezing her eyebrows overzealously.

I stared at the miniature well in the plastic.

It was supposed to take a few minutes to turn colours.

"Stop tweezing!"

I stared at the stick. The first hue was faint violet.

"Do you see anything?" she asked, still tweezing. Her eyebrows were getting thinner and thinner.

"Not really." I scrutinized the violet. "Take it easy on your poor eyebrows."

"What do you mean, not really, what the hell is it?"

"Well, the first hint of colour is a bit violet. I'm not sure what it means. Isn't violet what you get when you mix purple and blue? Maybe it means maybe. But anyways, we're supposed to wait five minutes, I think it's only been two point five minutes."

Isobel scrambled for the instructions, puffing on her smoke.

Three minutes could change everything in such a massive way. So many problems. The Proclaimers' song "500 Miles" started playing on the radio, and we sang out loud, pledging our love to each other in thick Scottish accents, trying to drown out the problem, knowing that when the song ended the stick would have a verdict. Tears streamed down Iz's face. Tears of the last days of freedom.

The song ended and morphed into the DJ's voice booming chatter.

I looked down at the stick. It was a red cross. It meant no. But, no, wait, didn't red mean alarm, emergency? "It's RED," I yelled before I could process what it meant for sure; stress had wiped out my short-term memory.

"Red?"

"Red!"

Isobel whooped and flapped her arms like she was a great crested crane.

"That's NO, right, red?"

"Uhh . . . uh . . . uhh . . . I . . ." My mind was stuck in a frozen panic, what did RED mean? My eyes scrambled through the directions.

"If you see a reddish cross YOU ARE NOT PREGNANT. YOU ARE NOT PREGNANT!" I read out loud.

"Woooooooooooooooooooooooo-hoooooooooooooooooooo ooooooooooooooooooo."

She was delirious, inventing a new kind of celebration dance. She threw her head around and shook her whole body like a woman taken by the power with an invisible hula hoop. I leaped out of the bath and joined in and danced my way over to the mini-bar. Normally a good idea to avoid the mini-bar's up-the-ass prices, but I took out the cheapest bottle. We chugged it back: syrupy Grand Marnier. All the muscles in my neck, my hands, my jaw, even my knees, unclenched. Isobel pretended the bed was a trampoline, leaping up and down in a liberation frenzy.

"I feel like making calls! Spreading the good news. Do you have any credit left on your calling card?" Isobel asked.

"Who were you thinking of calling?"

"I don't know. I guess it'd be rude leaving a message for Finn or Hubert like, 'Hey, pal, congratulations: you're not going to be the father of my child?'"

"Isobel. No. Let's just dance."

Sweaty and elated we resumed jumping and hollering in our newly invented Not-Preggers Waltz to the Tragically Hip singing "The Hundredth Meridian." Finally, we headed downstairs to the hotel lounge. It was a sad sight, but nothing out of the usual for karaoke lounges. We were so relieved and wanting to celebrate it didn't matter where we were. The bar was decorated in faux-ranch style with fake wood panelling, with the requisite deer head mounted above the bar. Business people sat around drinking Labatt Blues and rye-and-Cokes, smoking aimlessly; a few plaid-wearing underaged-looking kids from the suburbs were shooting stick. Like all karaoke bars it had the men, the men with the desperation, mired in nostalgia and yearning. Fifty-year-olds with plenty of passion who, once they get the mike in their hands, belt it out for Canada and for all their thwarted loves and hopes. Like the one on stage that night, Elvis hair with lambchop sideburns and a belly full of pathos and passion. The next up wore an orange Hawaiian shirt, and he keened away to the Beach Boys' "California Girls."

We sat down as far away from the singing as possible. I said to the bartender, thinking of *Withnail and I*: "We want the loveliest wines available to all of humanity and we'd like them now please!" He smiled but didn't move. After scanning the cocktail list, Isobel ordered us two screwdrivers. He poured us generous shots, apologizing for the lack of grand crus and pink champagne.

Shame and tackiness were thick in the smoky air of this nowhere karaoke bar in a town with a bad reputation for stranding hitchhikers. The vibe was familiar, like the one you get at a bingo parlour, or bowling—subcultures are full of weirdoes unless you're one of them. But who cared after what we'd been through, at least there was an atmosphere. Some hotel lounges have nothing going on, no aesthetic effort expended other than beer posters with football-breasted women in bathing suits.

"Wow, I feel so light. No more guilt and fear and loathing!"

"Ya, let's toast to no little Huberts! Thank Christ . . . Why *did* you have another fling with him anyway? I thought you were through with him years ago."

"It was a pride thing. I wanted to show him how I'd grown up and become such a femme fatale since we split. I was hoping he would grovel, so I could laugh at him. I thought I could wow him with my nonchalance, but he managed to out-aloof me. No more, I tell you, jamais!"

"Tchin tchin," we clanged our glasses together.

"Could we have two more, doubles, pease, we're celebating!" I slurred to the moustachioed bartender.

Round four convinced me that the deer on the wall was our new guardian angel. "No really, look Isobel, look at its eyes, it's watching us!"

On stage, a woman with a truly lovely voice was singing Patsy Cline's "Fall to Pieces." Behind her there was a five-foot screen playing a cheesy video accompanying the song with lyrics written to follow along on the bottom of the screen. A white ball bounced over the words as the song went on and the audience joined in. The format hadn't altered since the 1980s. A real show-woman, she clenched her fists in the air and fell to the ground, pretending she was literally falling too pieces. A table of supporters sitting as near as possible to the stage cheered and hollered as she hit and held the notes. The woman deserved a record contract.

Isobel sang along to "I fall to pieeeeces" with the woman and the other drunks. We clicked glasses almost every few sips. The sweet, massive relief of not being pregnant was almost worth the pregnancy scare itself. I felt as if I had almost been pregnant too. The orange juice swirled with the ice cubes and vodka. People say you can't taste vodka, but if you just put in enough, you can. Once you get past its medicinal taste, you can learn to like the kick, the bite, the sting, the kerpow factor. Plus, you can feel good about the fact that you are replenishing the vitamin C deficiency you get from smoking.

"Two please," I asked the bartender.

"Two what, eh?"

"Two, ugh, you know, dinks, drinks, I mean, drinks . . . please . . ." I can't believe I just said dinks. Oh my God. Mortification seared through my tipsiness.

"What kind of drinks?"

What was this, rocket science? "Two cocktails!" God, did I just overemphasize the Cock syllable. Oh man. I tried to give him my best sober look as Isobel pretended she was Edith Piaf beside me. Was he being coy or was this a test?

"So, any kind of cocktails, eh? I'm sorry, pardon me, I suffer from short-term memory loss." A fellow dope smoker maybe.

"Screwdrivers! Screwdrivers!" I yelled with glee, remembering what they were called.

"Coming right up," he said as he poured doubles for us.

I smiled a bit too much at him in gratitude and general drunken goodwill, then worried I was careening us toward another pregnancy scare. I stirred my drink, took a big gulp, felt a rush to my head from the coldness of the ice, and took another big swig to distract me from the frozen-brain feeling. Now my mouth was entirely frozen. On further scrutiny, I saw that the bartender looked a bit like Tom Selleck, which brought back fond memories of *Magnum P.I.* and the outfit I used to wear especially for watching his show when I was thirteen and even goofier than now. I smiled at him and passed Iz her drink. She was busy singing along with an old guy to Stompin' Tom Connors's song about snowmobiles.

"Here's to singleness, no kids!" she said, clashing her drink into mine so enthusiastically OJ spilled onto my T-shirt. I went stumbling off to the bathroom to do damage control on the stain. I only had three T-shirts for the trip and this was my favourite one. Pale blue, it said, VIRGINIA IS FOR LOVERS on it. I don't know why I liked it so much, I'd never been to Virginia. I wobbled down two flights of stairs, careful to clutch the handrail the whole way down. The bathroom looked pretty clean. There was a lurid arrangement of fake flowers and some more squirrel art on the walls. I was conscious of swaying a bit on my feet, but being a successful drinker means being able to function like normal. It just takes focus.

I looked in the mirror and was amazed by how puffy my eyelids looked and how mussed up my hair was. I tried to straighten my part with my finger. It wouldn't go like I wanted it to, so I doused it with water and tried to slick it down. The water felt good on my forehead. I splashed my face and neck with it, then bent over to take a long gulp.

I moistened a paper towel, pumped lots of soap on it, and scrubbed away at the OJ stain. I quickly lost patience with the soap and paper; the soap wouldn't stop foaming and I had millions of tiny fragments of paper towel stuck to my T-shirt. It looked like the Milky Way. I got compulsive and wet more paper towels and tried to clean up all the paper debris. Yet the more I wiped and wet it, the worse it got. Pretty soon I was going to look like I was the winner of a wet T-shirt contest.

Stop it, Annie, stop it. I closed my eyes and counted to five and then left the bathroom.

I think it was two pear ciders later, I felt so happy I could barely see. The bar seemed less full of people and all the ones who remained looked friendly and beautiful. I loved them all. And I loved Isobel. And I loved the bartender. I felt very warm. Tom was beautiful. Hawaii was so nice.

I adored the deer on the wall.

I loved coasters and peanuts and even smoke in my eye was only mildly annoying.

It seemed only right to grab the microphone and hand it to Isobel. She let me drag her to the stage. I couldn't get over how outrageous it was that there were no Hawksley songs on the machine. What kind of hick-ass place were we in? I looked around the swirling happy room and said to Iz, "Let's sing 'Safe and Sound,' we can do it!" With no karaoke machine, no amplification, just the volume of our hearts we did. I was so enthusiastic, it felt almost holy, singing my heart out in that dingy bar. After we finished one song, two shots of tequila arrived. With Isobel at my side I felt I could do anything. We were a unit. And I was protected. I don't know how many Hawksley songs we sang and tequilas we shot before I vomited, stage left, and Isobel fell down laughing.

The next morning I had a serious pasty mouth, a dry throat, and an African drum version of "Safe and Sound" pounding through my head. But I remembered the thrill of performing and I had vague memories of *Magnum P.I.* carrying first me fireman-style over his shoulder to the room, then Isobel. I scanned the room just to make sure neither of us had accidentally seduced him. Isobel was weighing herself. Since when did hotels have scales in them, I wondered. Unless she'd brought it with her. I closed my eyes.

We left the hotel at noon. I slapped the whole bill on my card, including the bar tab. I was paranoid that everything about me smelled like vomit, but I felt oddly confident that changing the tire should be in the realm of our capabilities, math failures or not. We could ride the high of not being pregnant for a long time. Hawksley was only one province away.

"... singing is about sexual confidence,
so sing out your guts if you feel good enough
to let the moment just hit you,
if the music befits you"
          "Paper Shoes," Hawksley Workman

By three o'clock I'd accepted that I was not getting the nuts on the tire to loosen. My hangover had overtaken my optimism. I was strong but annoyingly not tough enough to get them loose. Isobel gave it a try once or twice when it was obvious that I was getting exasperated. Every young woman should be able to do this—my mom could do it, I'd seen her do it. Smudges of grease on her face, she wasn't going to wait around for a man. I wish I hadn't been so busy rebelling against her and instead had learned this kind of valuable stuff. Like how to make her unbelievably delicious plum tart, sew buttons on leather jackets, and how in the heck to do an oil change and change a spare tire when the nuts were sealed too tight. *Bolts not nuts, Annie, don't be crude*, I could hear her saying.

Isobel flagged down a chortling old truck full of Mexicans. She didn't waste her time using her thumb, just some old-fashioned coquettish manoeuvre like Claudette Colbert in *It Happened One Night*. A little smile. A little thigh. A little thrusting of the lips and hips.

We could tell they were Mexicans because of the flag painted on the side of the rusty orange truck and the rosaries and plastic Virgin Marys swinging from the rear-view mirror. Three of them got out and cracked jokes while making quick work of the tire changing. Our replacement tire wasn't in great shape, the one named Pedro pointed out. Isobel smiled winningly and practised her self-taught French-style Spanish. Grande probleme, n'est-ce pas? No habla mucho Española. They were enchanted. They told us they were migrant workers on their way to pick Ontario tomatoes. Seemed like a helluva long way to come to pick tomatoes, but they were cheerful as all heck.

I smoked my last cigarette and by accident caught the eye of the guy still sitting in the truck, the anti-social one. He gave me a lazy, conspiratorial smile. I smiled back knowingly without exactly knowing what we were smiling about. Mexicanos are so beautiful with their golden brown skin, chocolate brown eyes, gleaming white teeth. Don Juanitos all of them, no matter if short or chubby, old or young, they've got twinkling eyes and are ready to flirt on the spot. Not to stereotype or anything.

No mucho Englese, they said, and it reminded me of our trip to Puerto Vallarta. Looking at these muchachos, I wanted to go back to Mexico, to travel with no sweetheart at home, free to roam. They are a kindred people, exceptionally romantic, like me. Always singing about love, talking about it hyperbolically.

I wondered why Philip, Marco, Pedro, and Guillermo were so far from home. I vaguely remembered hearing about migrant workers picking fruit, I guess they were trying to make a buck to take back to their families.

We thanked them, and Isobel gave them her email address. She drove us to the nearest garage. We bought a second-hand tire, loaded up with gas, bought some cigarettes, a green-apple-scented air freshener, some hand cream, red and black licorice, a bag of Spitz, and some ChapStick.

Isobel slapped her VISA card down on the counter. The red-headed and -bearded clerk swiped it, and we waited for it to be accepted and the little piece of paper to chit-chit out. It took longer than normal to work. The beeps sounded different. Red shook his head and whispered to us what the screen said: CARD NOT AUTHORIZED. Iz laughed nonchalantly and put her second card down, her MasterCard. No go. Red shook his head again. We'd been through this before, back when we were students. Her laugh sounded more hysterical this time round. My stomach rumbled.

I put my second credit card down, my VISA. I knew my MasterCard was jam-packed.

All three of us stared at the little black machine that would decide our fate.

No joy.

Isobel asked: Do you take department store cards? The guy shook is head. Gas cards? Aha, she said: my second VISA. We waited, holding our breath while he swiped it.

NOT AUTHORIZED! And I'm gonna have to confiscate this card, the guy said unhelpfully. Isobel tried to give him the fake Tag Heur Hubert had given her. Only an expert could tell it wasn't the real thing. This guy was thoroughly uninterested in her watch and treated us like bimbos; it wasn't like in the movies where you could make some sort of deal, like an IOU letter. He insisted on keeping our car as collateral until we could pay for our bill. Who knew Ontarians could be such hardasses? Sure, all of our credit cards had been declined, but we weren't riffraff! I knew from waitressing that you could just ring through a credit card manually, without calling VISA, and if it was under one hundred bucks, VISA would honour it because the customer would pay their bill eventually.

Red was unimpressed by my inside knowledge. "Maybe that's what you do in Alberta, that lawless province, but here in Ontario, we like to play by the book, eh."

I don't know if Red was being ironic or what, but screw him anyway. Isobel and I were experiencers, not savers. Go Hard or Go Home. This was our anthem. But now we had no wheels, no bucks, and we were stuck in a province that started with a vowel and ended in one but wasn't our Alberta.

I couldn't call my parents—I wouldn't—I didn't want a lecture on living beyond my means. Of all the lectures, that was my least favourite. What about my dreams, I'd argue back. Isobel's parents had already given her three hundred bucks for the trip. Who knew that gasoline could cost so goddamned much! We could call Finn, he would for sure help us out, but that would be so wrong on so many levels. Between us, we had ten bucks left. We could maybe hitchhike to Montreal, but we couldn't just abandon my car in Ontario. Plus, we needed to be able to get home. We walked the rainy streets of Wawa, destitute and lame. At least Red had let us leave our luggage there so we didn't have to schlepp it around town. Almost made up for him confiscating my keys.

It was a pretty place with loads of beaches around and an amazing super-hero-sized Canada Goose statue. I could add that sighting to the world's largest perogy I saw in Glendon, Alberta, a few years back.

"Aw merde alors, let's go to a movie, this is depressing!"

I loved that Isobel wanted to spend the last of our cash on a movie.

"Matinees are cheaper anyway, aren't they?"

So we found the local art-house cinema, but it wasn't open yet.

Needing to revive ourselves we headed to the grungiest bar we could find.

It had cheap decor of dark grey and black upholstered couches and ratty chairs stained from years of beer spillage. Mysterious abstract paintings of ominous blobs that looked like crows hung on the walls. Hundreds of empty beer pitchers sat stacked on the bar, for the evening ahead. Our table had a plastic black ashtray with an old butt squashed into a piece of green bubblegum on it along with one of the neon yellow flyers that lay on every table advertising The Hard Rock Miners.

On the back of our flyer we made a list of our options: *camp, hitchhike, make friends.* Fuzzy Navels and extra spicy chicken wings were on special, so we went for broke. Two Fuzzy Navels later, with my peach schnapps wisdom, I had written a postcard to Finn, asking him to get me an advance at work on my paycheque. They'd done it before. My bosses were good guys, fairly tolerant of their young staff's dramas. Isobel had a stamp left in her wallet and went off to post it.

Later on after endless noodling and wandering around, we found a park and sat on a bench. I felt bad for Isobel. She looked a little demoralized as she fished in her bag for cigarettes. There was nothing to do but sleep in the park, like a couple of hobos. We lay head to toe on the long bench.

"Isobel, this is just like a Tom Waits song, we're actually living it."

"I'd rather just hear about it in a song."

"What song?"

"'Cold Cold Ground'?"

Thank God it was a warm summer night.

It was four in the morning and here we were on a bench in small-town Ontario. At least it would make a good story. At least we were having an adventure. And then the rain started. I heard Isobel say Zut! She put her purse on her face to shield herself from the drops.

I let it splatter on my face. It was only a gentle rain. I imagined I was kissing Hawksley, and we were laughing in retrospect over my epic mission to get to him. We were a couple. Madly in love. Having sex at every possible, sneaky chance. Kissing in car washes.

He was busy with his rock-star lifestyle. But he made time for me. He needed me. I inspired him. I was the listener he'd longed for, his muse. And so we smooched and smooched.

Woke up five hours later. Nine in the morning and only a buck fifty between us. Hungry bellies, full bladders, and damp clothes from dew and drizzle.

Isobel looked gorgeous as usual, despite having slept in these conditions. She looked in her compact mirror and cleaned up her eye makeup, brushing on more mascara and slapping on some lipgloss. I looked in my mirror. I had bench imprints on the left side of my face. There was a weird look in my eyes. I snapped the mirror shut.

We walked back into town looking for somewhere to eat and pee. It was a sunny, blue-sky day. I didn't know how we were going to get to Hawksley in Montreal in two days' time, but I had hope. How could you not, on such a beautiful day? I ignored the tickle in my throat that hinted at a cold on the way.

"Do you think we should just go home?" Isobel asked.

My heart sank. We'd never given up on a mission. The thought that she didn't want to carry on made me feel desperately sad. Down I went into a pit of self-loathing and pity pity pity.

"Annie?"

I looked at her, trying to suss out whether she was fed up with our mission. "I'd really like to see him, Iz. I really would. I know it's stupid, but I think he could change my life."

"Okay then, let's do it! Oui. We'll find a way. Let's go to that café over there. It looks nice."

"We don't have any money, Isobel. Remember, *all* of our credit cards are up to their limits."

"Look, we'll go in, order food, use the bathrooms, eat, and then we'll be able to think clearly, I don't know, maybe they don't have a VISA authorization machine, maybe they just imprint the cards. We'll case it on the way in. Baby steps. Petits pas."

I didn't really think it was a good idea. I didn't want to get sent to the clink in small-town Ontario. Plus I was a waitress, I had honour. I couldn't possibly do a dine and dash, the last refuge of the lowest of the low.

But I was hungry and I had to pee like crazy, so I acquiesced.

I waited at our table while Iz went to the can first. I saw her looking all around the place, trying to figure out what their credit card payment situation was. It was a tiny café painted a light lemony colour. Blond wood tables. Georgia O'Keefe prints on the walls. Fresh orange tiger lilies in a vase on top of the cake display. A bookshelf overflowing with paperbacks with a sign above saying, TAKE ONE, LEAVE ONE. A menu written in electric blue chalk.

There were a lot of customers: a smattering of twenty-somethings, families, a few professor-looking types. Isobel came back and it was my turn to go and freshen up. "Did you see a machine?"

"No, it's too cluttered by the till to really see anything."

She was right, the till area had dirty plates all around it. It was an impromptu bus station for what looked like a large party that had just left. Weird that this place was so busy at nine-thirty on a Wednesday morning.

I came back to the table, and we scanned the menu. I felt better after having brushed my teeth and hair and put on some lipstick. My stomach was worried, wondering how we were going to pay for this, but my appetite was blithely panoramic.

Isobel was annoyed that the place was non-smoking. I thought it was good for us to have to conserve our supplies.

The menu seemed way more sophisticated than anything back home. I felt that my body might even forgive all the debauchery if I cleansed it with this healthy food. I ordered a fruit soup of puréed cantaloupe, nectarine, and raspberries, a tofu and veggie bacon English muffin, and gyokuru Japanese tea to drink. Isobel ordered pan-fried portobello mushrooms filled with organic pesto and caramelized shallots.

"What a menu!"

"I think this place must be for vegans, I just wanted some damn eggs," said Isobel.

I was so hungry I felt faint.

Just then, we overheard the waitress say to another customer, "We don't accept credit cards here. Sorry, there's a bank machine around the corner."

"What are we going to do?" I whispered.

"I know for sure there's no money in my account, or yours, is there?"

"Nope."

"Maybe we can argue about the fact that we didn't know."

The waitress arrived with our food. It looked beautiful.

"Sorry I just overheard, you don't do credit cards? In this day and age?"

I cringed from the rudeness of Iz's tone. The waitress sighed. "Look, these credit card companies charge a huge fee for us to be able to use them, and for a small place like this, with gourmet food at reasonable prices for the customer, we just don't want to pass on the costs to you, so we thought, 'Hey let's simplify this, let's be old-fashioned and just use cash.'" And she walked off.

Isobel snorted. "Well, it looks like we might have to do a runner."

How horrible is that? In this nice place. I put the first spoonful of soup in my mouth. It was a kind of heaven. Beautiful fruity, tangy flavours erupted in my mouth. I had a sip of the tea, that was delicious too. I leaned across the table and even had a piece of Iz's mushroom. Wow.

"Let's just eat first. Then we'll worry. Meanwhile this is the healthiest food we've had this whole trip. Think of all those Husky greasy-sausage–fried-egg assembly-line breakfasts." As I said that, I noticed a blond man in his early fifties sitting at the table next to us, peering over the book he was reading, which was something about eco-criticism.

"Sorry for being so terribly rude, but I couldn't help overhearing your conversation. Since I've been here, I've been dying to have some classic, greasy-spoon breakfast like you see in American cinema but to no avail. Do you know of such diners in town? I'm dying for a steak 'n' eggs breakfast!"

He had a BBC accent, which of course made us both sit up in our chairs. He must be an expert of something.

"Well, if you get out of town to the highway, you should be able to find a Husky. But it's nothing special," I told him.

"Do they give you endless coffee refills, in fact leaving a thermos on your table?"

"Sure do, and there's a phone on every table so that truckers can call their wives," Isobel added.

"Thanks for the tip."

"Are you from England?" I couldn't believe I'd just said that, of course he was.

"Yes indeed, I'm a Somerset man."

"Like Sting, and Tears for Fears, Peter Gabriel and Joe Strummer and Van Morrison sometimes and . . ."

"Yes, it's an attractive region. Draws a lot of rock stars and birdwatchers, burnt-out Londoners and farmers. Gabriel's 'Solsbury Hill,' I go there all the time for picnics."

He couldn't have impressed us more.

He was hugely boyish despite being in his fifties. Super red-faced, very fair. Looking like he might burst somehow. I hoped Isobel wouldn't try to seduce him, just for sport. He looked vulnerable. And sweet. The more he talked, the more it made me think of George Emmerson, cups of tea, Billy Idol, crumpets, and all good things English.

"So, I really am not generally an eavesdropper, but how about we create a diversion for your little problem," he suggested.

"I don't know, I don't feel right about it, I work in restaurants."

"Oh . . . I took you for radicals, bohemians, revolutionaries. Isn't property theft? . . ."

"Well—"

"Okay, when you're done eating, on the count of four, I'll spill my coffee and you two get up and leave. Don't look suspicious, just head out the door as if you'd already paid. I'll meet you around the corner."

Pretending to try to scratch his ear, he swiped his coffee cup, spilling it all over the table. To make matters worse he instinctively jumped up to avoid the lake of coffee but managed to tip the table so all the coffee spilled over his lap definitely making a bigger mess than he'd intended. It was an incredible act of kindness, I thought as we walked casually out of the place.

We hid around the corner. He came out in a few minutes.

"That was just like in the movies!"

This guy had a bad case of movie-itis, I figured, possibly worse than ours.

"I don't feel good about this, I gotta go back and confess." I stormed back in. "Wait—" I heard behind me.

When I walked up to the counter I said to the woman that I had forgotten to pay and I was sorry. Before I could start my negotiations of how I might pay, she said, "Don't worry about it, honey, that English dude paid your tab."

Gobsmacked, as they say in England. That's what I was.

"Kerridge," he said, "pleased to meet you both! Mind if I walk with you?"

We headed back to our bench. Along the way, we told him our story, the Hawksley mission, the mushrooms, Rosimund in captivity, Sullivan, Finn, Ani DiFranco, and a little about Hubert. He told us he was a visiting professor/poet here for two months to host a spoken word festival at the local arts centre. He was here to slam poetry!

"My God, you girls are living in a Don Quixote saga. He expected the inn he stayed in to accept his credit, but they wouldn't. You're sort of on this *Thelma and Louise* homoerotic psychedelic landscape picaresque of the big Wild Wild West/ East. Yes, of course, of course—this is too perfect . . ."

His eyes looked dreamy, maybe he was composing one of his poems about us.

"So you're saying we're a couple of sirens?" Isobel asked.

"Well that's one way of putting it. So tell me, what's the next chapter of your saga, how are you planning to get to Montreal? I'd drive you myself, but I need to be hosting this poetry-off. I could give you some cash, I've got fifty quid in my pocket."

"Whoa, monsieur! No way, no how. We're adults, we need to find a decent way to get ourselves out of this mess that doesn't include les shenanigans with older British men!" Isobel laughed.

"Do you have anything you could sell or pawn?"

"We just have our car, and Finn's guitar and we can't sell that," I said.

"Why would you sell it? You could busk! Of course, that's it . . ."

"We are *huge* music appreciators, Isobel and I, not musical at all sadly . . ."

"I'll help, we'll busk together! Seriously, it's a great way to make a quick buck. I haven't done it in years, but I'm sure it still works the same."

This was just so weird. A fifty-year-old English man trying to convince a couple of twentysomethings to busk. Even more weirdly, I was up for it. "Whatta we got to lose?" I realized.

"Dignity," Isobel answered.

"Oh c'mon, no one knows us here in this town. Look, Isobel, it'll be just like karaoke, only with more creative freedom. Please."

We headed to the gas station to get the guitar from the backseat of the car. I worried about the potential bad scene awaiting us back at the station, but Kerridge said he would tell Red he'd vouch that we would be back to pay the bill.

"These two minstrels here are going to give an amazing concert this afternoon that you really shouldn't miss. Main Street in three hours," he told the bored clerk.

So we headed back to the park. I was glad I'd had the cantaloupe soup, but I was still a little hungry. The sun was really in full form, beating down on our heads. Luckily there were giant, old maple trees lining the streets giving us some relief.

It happened so quickly I didn't have time to warn them.

Something was tickling my nose. I opened an eye, Isobel was tickling me with a blade of grass. Kerridge was holding my wrist, checking my pulse. They stood me up and walked me over to a water fountain. He wanted to know if this was normal behaviour for me, sudden drops to the ground. I told him yes.

After the water I felt better. I needed more food. We went into a 7-Eleven and he bought me a hamburger in a bag that we nuked in the microwave. I ate that in two seconds. He bought me another, and he and Iz had one each. God bless North America, he said as he got us a round of lime-flavoured Slurpees and a couple of lottery scratch cards.

Isobel used the 7-Eleven bathroom to change into a red dress she had got out of her bag from the car when I was busy negotiating with Red. She came back looking like a Spanish diva. I was as jealous as usual of her perfection. She handed me a bandana.

"That's it?" I asked.

"Eh ben dis-donc, you're not really one for dressing up, are you?"

I was annoyed. She always got to be the goddamn beauty queen. I tied the blue and white bandanna around my neck, trying to feel rock 'n' roll, but felt more like an angry punk. It was the wrong vibe. We sat in the hot sun, waiting for Kerridge, who was using the bathroom. I put on some more lipgloss and some shimmering eyeshadow to soften my look. At least I was wearing a decent gypsy cotton top with my best pair of cutoff shorts. Isobel trumped everything by taking off her bra, saying she was too hot. Next you thing you know, she'd be pouring water down her dress.

"Let's go find a good bench. We need to work on our shtick," Kerridge said.

He didn't seem to be ogling her obvious nipples. After we'd scratched our tickets and won nothing, we brainstormed for an hour going through all of our favourite songs, singers, lyrics. Kerridge practised on the guitar and managed to perfect a two-chord riff that he figured we could use all day. He taught me it, and my fingers struggled to bend in the right way. I figured I could ultimately go in for loud and vigorous strumming, doing only the most basic chord progressions. Isobel shook the ice in her Slurpee for a percussive element. This inspired Kerridge to go on a mission to find a pawn shop to get a tambourine.

He came back singing "A Day in the Life"; he was thoroughly embracing the adventure. Super keener. Not only had he scored a tambourine but also a Beatles songbook in the adjacent music store.

My doubts about the success of our busking were so enormous I'd been trying to come up with other ways to get our car out of hock and get us to Montreal. Selling the guitar wasn't really an option, that would just be appalling, considering the autograph and Finn's gesture. My grandmother's opal ring was my prize possession and not an option. I couldn't bear phoning my family and feeling like a schmuck. Maybe I could phone VISA and get my credit limit extended . . .

We decided on doing Beatles' songs because we had the book and also partly in honour of Kerridge's Britishness, and also—who doesn't love the Beatles! Plus, when I sing along to their music I actually feel like I'm doing it right.

I obviously couldn't really play the guitar properly, so Kerridge was to be the guitarist, me the percussionist, and Isobel the front woman. We had the book open on the grass in front of us, and if we stood in a horizontal line, we could pretty much all read it. The book turned out to be just a prompt really, lyric-wise, because those lyrics seemed already naturally emblazoned on our psyches. We practised two goes of the book. From "Oh bla di o bla da" to my personal favourite, "Amsterdam."

It was so much fun to be in the middle of small-town Ontario with this crazy Brit, jamming. We were jamming! Kerridge and I alternated between the guitar and the tambourine, while Isobel jiggled and sang like a cockatoo. We practised for a couple of hours. He told us stories from when he was our age in the 1970s. How he'd worn purple pants and orange tops and gotten arrested for doing acid and roaming around an owl sanctuary in Sussex. How he went bird watching with his older sister and lost their money in the woods and how they had to busk in a small, posh village just to get enough money for the train fare home and how they hitched a ride home in the end with hippies who smoked them up. One guy had question marks on the front of his sunglasses. It also sounded so romantic, like *A Room with a View* fused with *Withnail and I.*

Surely we could make up for our lack of technique or polish, in fact our whole raw thing, with sheer summertime enthusiasm. We jammed until it was time to scout our location. Downtown in the main square there were some real musicians so we went away from the centre where we found a lane that had three coffee shops with patios full of mostly empty tables except for a couple of readers. It was two o'clock, people reluctantly strolling back toward their offices.

"Ladies and gentlemen, please bear with us. We are a new band. Very new indeed. Blushingly new. So forgive us our transgressions. We hope it isn't too painful." Kerridge said his piece, then backed up into formation with us. I felt sick, queasy. There were only three people sitting on the four patios. Did Dan Bern feel this way? Hawksley? Ani?

"Right girls, imagine we're in Paris in the 1960s, Situationists, rebelling against elitism, reclaiming our right to be artists!" And with that he launched into "Paperback Writer." I didn't need to look down at the sheets. No, it wasn't remembering the lyrics, it was the sound of our voices that freaked me out. I tried to move my body in a dancing kind of way. Two people from the patio got up and left. With the sun beaming down on my face and just the one guy there busy reading a newspaper, I felt my self-consciousness start to slide away. When the reader got up to go to the bathroom, Kerridge chucked a five-dollar bill and a handful of loonies in the guitar case.

"Monkey see, monkey do, works every time."

So we sang and we sang for an hour and by that time we'd perfected some of the songs. We were now competent on "Paperback Writer," "Revolution," and a medley of five other songs. The waiters and waitresses were finishing their lunchtime shifts and their replacements were strolling on in. Some smiled as they passed us, a few tossed in coins.

We smiled back. All of us. Big. The Beatles were obviously a massive crowd pleaser even from our bumbling selves. And there were some points where I felt like Kerridge and I actually reached some gorgeous-sounding McCartney/Lennon harmonies.

It was four o'clock and my throat was sore, but a pile of money was growing in our case. I couldn't believe it. We were halfway through the songbook. (We had to skip any of the more experimental songs; they were just too tricky.)

The patios slowly started filling up again for Happy Hour. Strawberry margaritas were being served and ice cold schooners of honey-coloured beer. Nachos dripping with sour cream and cheddar cheese and guacamole plunked in the middle of truly happy people. There was other music playing on café stereos, but not so loud, and people still seemed to be enjoying us. In fact, the longer Happy Hour went on, the more beer was guzzled, the more applause we got. Gooners sang along with us.

One sly waiter brought us what looked to be coffees to go but turned out to be beer! I sang and sang and shook that tambourine for all I was worth. Kerridge was thrilled banging away on the guitar. He was even redder in the face than before, and I was worried that delicate English skin of his might be getting burned. Isobel was happily strutting around as if she was dancing in the shower, belting it out.

The sun pelted down on me, and the beer collided with sun spots; we bellowed "Love Love Me Do." I felt love and forgiveness. As if I could ever stay cranky at this girl, this co-pilot of my life. What a muchacha she was! I was proud. We were a great team, the best buddy sisterhood. Forget Danny Glover and Mel Gibson. We were way closer. Thelma and Louise, the Golden Girls, Laverne and Shirley.

We didn't wrap it up until just after midnight when last call had come and gone for the patio and people had gone inside to finish drinking. We walked inside the first one and got more applause. It was really a bit embarrassing. They gave us a pizza on the house, and we counted our earnings: one hundred and fifty buckeroos!!!! Kerridge insisted we keep it all.

"That was so brilliant! I'm reliving the youth I never had. I always dreamed of being a musician in America."

"This is Canada."

"Sorry, yes yes, of course."

We would be able to pay off the gas station bill, get the car out of hock, and have ninety bucks left over for gas, it was a great start to fiscal rectitude and recovery. Amazing. And we'd earned it ourselves. Finn would be so proud. And God how I'd loved being in the middle of the music and not just watching it. It was a high I hadn't experienced since I did that air-guitar performance of Frankie Goes to Hollywood's "Relax" at talent night in Grade 4.

After the bar finally closed, we were still all high from our day as rock stars. Kerridge said he had a vw van he'd rented that was parked on a campsite in front of a lake near town. He said it was a birdwatchers' paradise. A free place to crash was a great bonus, so we all piled into a taxi to drive us out there.

Inside the green van was a shambolic arrangement of

piles of books and binoculars and poems written on Post-it notes attached to the walls. Beside a picture of an Ontario green tit, he had a quotation from Emily Dickinson: "If I feel physically as if the top of my head were taken off, I know that is poetry."

We made a fire on the lakefront and toasted the Beatles and talked and talked. And smoked a little pot. He talked about England and E.M. Forster and D.H. Lawrence and Thomas Hardy, and we listened to him rhapsodize late into the night about the North American robin versus its tiny English counterpart and Canada in general as a hotbed of not just culture but hummingbirds too. He was so goddamned enthusiastic for life, it was fun just to be around him. And he had a big brain. A big English brain.

"Though I am a doctor of literature, and not a doctor doctor, I do have a hunch about your lapses in consciousness, young Annie. Let me feel your pulse."

I gladly gave him my wrist. He was my new guru.

"Yes, I thought so, you've got low blood pressure. And dope, well I'm afraid you'll need to cut it out, your pulse is slower than after you fainted. Annie, you need to take actual care of yourself, you are a beautiful young woman with such a life ahead of you." He was quoting my mother.

"You also need to pursue this music thing, rather than just the musicians. It'll be good for your health! If you take singing lessons, they will teach you how to breathe properly."

Isobel spoke up. "C'mon, Kerridge, you're bullshitting. A slow pulse does not mean low blood pressure! I failed math, but I do know that."

"Okay, that's true, but singing lessons would definitely help. Go forth, you young women, conquer the road, bring that Hawksley to his knees with your obvious charms! And try to ease off the hedonism, just a little."

In my post-busking euphoria and stonerness, his one-liner solutions for my life felt like the most genius wisdom I'd ever heard. There was no way we were going to sleep that night. It was so light out, we just kept talking bullshit. He was over the top with his take on us: "You're rebels, you're outsiders—practically lesbians, for all intents and purposes, rejecting men and seeking life and art on your own terms, grabbing the balls of your own adventure, saying 'up yours' to suburbia, to empty consumerism and, goodness gracious, to Céline Dion, you are like the first great women pioneers. Reject the status quo, embrace all experience! God, I wish I was your age again! Let me tell you, I'm not bullshitting you, as you would say: this trip, these kind of times are the times that will live on in your life well after it's over and winter has come and you've got arthritis. You are living!! And you must, must, must do more canoeing! Absolutely, this is the Canadian advantage, all the canoeing opportunities that simply don't exist in Britain. They just don't . . ."

"Oh la la, you're really stoned!" Isobel said.

I was with him on his same infectious wavelength. We ate hot dogs at four in the morning. By six, we were delirious. Fish were jumping, birds had woken up and were in the midst of their dawn chorus. We decided to go skinny dipping in the lake as the sun rose.

I swam underwater and surfaced again and dove down again like a dolphin—I felt strong. Kerridge swam along beside us, doing his own aquatic whoops.

I made vows to myself at this new dawn. No more Sullivan, no more dope, no more smokes, less decadence. Just the beautiful dawn. And my best friend and new guru. What could be better?

Now I could meet Hawksley as more of an equal, a fellow troubadour. And Springsteen, Bruce Springsteen. Kerridge said life is all two steps forward, one step back, and if I needed advice from now on, listen to Springsteen, dammit.

We crashed asleep for a few hours on the floor of the van.

"I'm invincible
so are you
we do all the things
they say we can't do
we walk around
in the middle of the night
and if it's too far to walk
we just hitch a ride
we got rings of dirt
around our necks
we talk like auctioneers . . .
we are wise wise women
we are giggling girls"
     "If He Tries Anything," Ani DiFranco

Day 7
+30 Celsius, blue sky with bonus:
super-sticky eastern humidity
drink index: Fuzzy Navel & Black Label beer
Poutine: Québécois number-one dish

3,326 km behind us
Wawa to Montreal
1,215 km to go

I stuck a Polaroid photo of Kerridge on the dash with a piece
of gum beside pics of Hawksley and a stick-on Buddha statue.

It was an epic driving day going along the coast of Lake Superior: down past Sault Ste. Marie, over to Sudbury and North Bay, down to Ottawa. We stopped for a few naps and snacks and pee breaks and stretching-our-legs breaks along the never-ending highway. At our last stop, we went off piste to go for a swim. It was super hot and sticky out and I thought it would be adventurous to go for a skinny dip, to keep up the new Kerridgean path of embracing everything in nature, particularly lakes, but Isobel got a bloodsucker on her nose and then I had to burn it off with a cigarette. So her nose swelled and chafed. She'd never had an ugly day before and wasn't happy about it.

I shouldn't have been pleased.

She was sulking and looking at herself in the rear-view mirror every five minutes to see if the swelling had gone down.

Many hours later, crossing the border from Ontario to Quebec, Isobel took a break from sulking to whoop and cheer with me. We belted out the traditional French beer anthem that we'd learned almost a decade before: "On est saoul, on est saoul, on est saoul l'effet de la bière!" Careening on and off of the rumble strips we sang the one and only verse in an endless loop, putting all of our operatic gusto into the hard-core Quebbie pronunciation of be-er. Isobel added, in her best Charles de Gaulle voice, "VIVE Le Québec Libre!"

I think being in Quebec makes people impulsive. I mean, there's something about Frenchness that just jazzes everything up. *Joie de vivre.* I blame what happened with Isobel and me that summer on the Québécois syndrome.

Besides being French and sexier than the rest of Canada,

for me and Isobel, Quebec symbolized an emotional land-mark—it marked the site of our very first romantic and boozy adventures. As we drove toward Montreal in silence, I looked at the Québécois licence plates ahead of us that said, JE ME SOUVIENS . . .

We were fifteen years old when we first set foot in French Canada. It was possibly the most exciting time of our collective lives up until that point—except for watching Live Aid on TV. Back at home we went to Catholic Separate High School. Separate really felt like a giant euphemism for Lame. We were pretty much sheltered from all the glories of public school culture that we had studied like anthropologists on TV. We drooled over the dating and partying scene that public school kids took for granted. We managed to get to be fifteen years old without having ever kissed boys, smoked drugs, or drunk beer. It wasn't due to some shortage of enthusiasm—we were dying to be corrupted.

Our big chance finally came when we signed up for a six-week course in Quebec where we would be, as the brochure explained: "immersed in French language and culture." The previous year's students called it Club Fed and assured us it was party central. The brochure promised we would: "live, sleep, and dream in French." Madame Plouffe, our French teacher, thought it was merveilleux that batches of franco-philes were hatched out of the program in six-week rotations.

Out of over a hundred students from all over the country, we were the youngest—there were even some twenty-year-olds in the program—and that made us feel unspeakably glamorous (relative to our peers back home) as well as slightly out of our league. But we knew how to bluff, especially Isobel.

Isobel was no longer a goofy young girl; she was a gorgeous teenager with a nice brown tan, those amazing green eyes, and Liquid Paper white teeth. She was tall and thin and her light brown hair was all one length but short-ish and parted to the side like she'd seen Ralph Lauren models do on *Fashion Files* on TV. I still had braces on my teeth and not a lot of confidence. Recently I'd given my image an overhaul and gotten rid of my Chrissie Hynde/footballer eye-makeup and Sid Vicious hairstyle; I felt a bit exposed without all the eyeliner and hair product, but I had to face the fact that real punk was way before my time and my parents wouldn't ever let me dye my hair blue anyway. Besides, punk boys don't necessarily go for punk girls. Look at Billy Idol's wives. Looking feminine felt pretty unnatural to me.

Montreal city, Dorval airport, was where the gong show began. We had to wait there for a couple of hours before taking a little plane up north. On the way to the Edmonton airport, Dad had said: "Now, girls . . . don't think you need to have a drink in the airport. There's no reason to go nuts now, just because you'll have no parental supervision for six weeks and you're going to a province with a more liberal approach to drinking ages. What I'm saying is: BEHAVE yourselves and don't act like WILD ANIMALS!"

Isobel figured out we had to go to Gate 10 to board the next plane in four hours, so we thought we'd follow Dad's advice and try our luck out at the lounge. We sat down, trying to look as sophisticated as possible. I kept my jacket on so they wouldn't see my Billy Idol White Wedding Tour T-shirt. I stopped smiling so nobody would see my braces. On our table beside the peanuts there was a card featuring a cocktail special: *Fuzzy Navel (Peach Schnapps and Orange Juice)*. The waitress didn't blink when we ordered a couple of those. They were fizzy, sweet, and delicious; we got wazooed pretty quickly. It was our first major drinking experience. At home we'd only sampled the odd beer or sipped our miniscule quota of Christmas cava.

Three hours later and three Fuzzy Navels each, we realized standing at Gate 10 that it was Gate 32a we needed to get to—it was obvious to me then how bad Isobel's French was (she'd been in charge of listening for the gate number while I was on peanut refill duty). We ran at least three laps around the airport: north, south, east, before running down the right conveyer belt. Hallelujah—drunk, huffing and puffing, we made it on to the little passenger plane: destination Jonquière!

Once on board, we sat in the last row. Right from the get-go, Isobel caught sight of her dream boy sitting adjacent to us in a window seat. He was sexy in that boy-who-listens-to-the-Smiths kind of way. He had tortoiseshell glasses, Jesus sandals, and a James Dean hairdo. He sat on my right and Isobel on my left. She spent the whole flight leaning forward, making me sit back so she could check him out at her leisure. I had a peach fuzzy headache and felt a little uncertain about everything up in the sky in our little tin can of an airplane.

In the Lac-Saint-Jean region in northern Quebec, Jonquière was not far from the aluminum capital of the world where they made ALCAN, the tin foil our moms used to wrap left-overs. The factory gave the area a smell that was noticeable right off the bat, a bit like the pulp mill pong in Hinton,

Alberta. On the plus side, it made for some crazy-gorgeous-coloured sunsets.

When we landed it was a rainy night and there were definitely no parents in sight. We took a taxi to the residence and checked in and dropped off our suitcases. After the success we had had at the airport ordering drinks, we figured we were brave enough to hit the streets of small-town Quebec.

Our first stop was at the dépanneur to buy some gum. I noticed right away that there was beer in the fridge. In Alberta adults had to go to a government store to buy booze. Unparalleled freedoms! Isobel brazenly walked over, opened the fridge, and picked up a couple of Budweisers. The guy at the counter was very friendly: "Salut, les filles? Ça bouge?"

"Uh, bouge?

"Et oui, Ça gaze?"

"Uh, oui . . . wee wee wee!"

"Ah, vous êtes des anglophones la! Pis ba . . . Je comprends . . . ow are you? You've just arrived ear in Quebeck and you tought you'd get some Buddy-wisers, asteur la, ahhhh!"

We laughed with the guy. He reminded me of my friendly postman from back home. I put the beers in my bag for later, and off we went clunking up the street. Chez Max's neon blue sign featuring a large-sized man with a chef's hat looked appealing as a first stop. We walked in and headed for a booth table. There was only one other customer in the six-table place: the James-Dean-hairdo guy from the plane.

We sat down at the booth beside his. Isobel was trying not to smile too much, but her voice had gone up three octaves: "Poutine, what's that, do you think?"

The waiter came up saying something about us being

square heads. "Poutine is de food of de people, it iz frites with fromage and sauce. It is essentiel for all Québéçois people."

"S'il vous-plaît, oui . . . Je suis nouveau ici . . . Je suis faim, eu, non J'AI faim!" I said.

The waiter walked away, shaking his head.

"What did he say was on top?" Isobel asked me.

"It's topped with squeaky cheese." The James-Dean-hairdo guy turned around. "Cheese curds from the region. This cheese is famous for squeaking when you put it in your mouth. Ça chante."

I found it hard to believe that cheese could squeak.

He held out his hand to shake mine and said, "Enchanté. Idaho."

"Nice to meet you too. Alberta."

Isobel elbowed me in the ribs. "It's his name, not where he's from."

"Idaho?"

My first Québécois morning I woke up sleeping top to tail with Isobel, with a pounding in my brain, feeling like an aluminum factory had been built on my head. There was also a dangerous rumbling in my guts. I looked down the bed to Izzy, who was holding her hand against her forehead. "Annie, a great illness has befallen me."

"Me too, girlfriend, me too. Good God! Maybe we got some kind of poisoning, maybe we got alcohol poisoning!"

"Don't exaggerate, c'mon. Oh God, do you think that's possible?"

"I hope they don't call our parents. They wouldn't do that, would they?"

"Or the police, 'cause we're underage?"

"No way. What's the bartender gonna say, Deez girlz ad two maybe tree Fuzzy Navels, pantoute!"

"Oh man, I think I gotta hurl."

"Hold it . . . maybe you just need some air."

"The main thing is not to panic."

We spent the morning outside the residence, lounging in the park trying not to vomit. We had to be at the orientation for the program at 5:00 PM. Other students played Frisbee and sat with their groups of friends. We made a list of modest goals for the summer:

French kiss at least one boy.

Try every kind of alcohol available.

Learn to be suave in French.

Absolutely no baiser-ing. (don't want to get pregnant!!!)

It was a hot July day and there were no mosquitoes. Idaho wandered along wearing sunglasses, a floral shirt, and cutoffs.

"Girls, what's the hangover index this morning? Mine's off the scales, those Fuzzy Navels you like to drink are nothing but sugar."

"It wasn't poisoning then? We don't have to get our stomachs pumped?!" I asked, despite knowing I was revealing nerdiness.

"Have some Gatorade, gotta replace your fluids. You don't go to the hospital for Gueule de bois—that's French for hangover, it means woody mouth," Idaho told us. He had been at this same program the year before and had a handle on the essentials—he was fast becoming our mentor.

I had blunt-length curly hair. The major bonus of my hairdo was if I had to, in an uncomfortable situation, I could untuck my hair from behind my ear and shield most of my face from vision. I needed to do that immediately when a

Frisbee landed near my foot and some guy ran up and plunked himself down to introduce himself. He was a preppie boy wearing desert boots, a cream-coloured cotton surfer hoodie, and an almost offensive amount of Polo cologne, every preppie's signature smell. He wasn't my preferred new-wave, punky type of guy, but he had the kind of blue eyes that people write songs about.

"Salut, je m'appèle Johnny. D'ou vous venez de . . . aw shit . . . I'm Johnny. Where are you guys from?"

"Alberta, Edmonton."

"Vous êtes des cowgirls?"

"Oui, oui, mon cheval est dans ma chambre," Isobel said.

"Et toi?" I managed to ask.

"Toronto. Me and those guys over there all go to the same school."

Isobel chatted nonchalantly with him, I hid behind my hair and tried to think of something to say. Everyone was speaking quietly in case there were any French spies around whose presence we'd been assured of.

"You like to Frisbee?" he asked me.

"Ya, you know, it's fun."

"Ya."

Oh man it was painful. Why had he sat down? When would he leave? Would he come back after he left? Isobel was so at ease. Unlike my mom, Isobel's liked to give boy advice. She had told her right before we left: "Now, Isobel, I want you to know, sometimes it happens that you meet a boy and maybe you spend a lot of time together and then maybe you start fooling around, with clothes on and maybe . . . you start to feel really good . . ."

"Mom?!"

"No, but seriously, I am no fool. Your mother understands these things. But the most important thing that I want you to remember is that before you go too far: think of me, think of my face. When you think you might lose control, imagine me."

I had never even gone to a spin-the-bottle party like I'd seen on TV. My whole romantic history consisted of that one-sided kiss with Mike the Spike. He basically planted one on me, and I was too stunned to respond, imagining Isobel's mother. I hadn't moved my lips at all, so he had never called me again. That was ten months ago. Since then I had read lots of divorcee romances that I borrowed from my mom's divorced friend. *Second Chance Romances* had given me a few ideas. I really wanted a second shot at it, vowing I would definitely kiss back this time round.

It was a major coup to score the hottest guy in the program; I have no idea how I did it. I think it was just geographical—I sat next to Johnny at Chez Max. He had four Old Stock 7% beers and then leaned over and kissed my cheek. "Let's hang out," he said.

Later that night, outside of the dormitory, we were the last two to go inside. It was twilight and we kicked off our shoes. He took my hand and walked me on to the grass to ballroom dance around the pine trees. My head rushed when he dipped me tango-style. Standing there with blades of grass tickling the skin between my toes, he put his finger under my chin and raised my mouth to his. He put his lips on mine. The stubble on his chin scraped my cheek, but his lips were warm and soft. I was ready to move my lips, determined not to relive the Mike the Spike routine. I banished Iz's mom from my brain, and I went for his lower lip and took it in between my lips. He giggled and then licked me lightly. I got my tongue out too. We touched tongues! Then I ventured my tongue into his mouth and tried to probe around like they described in the romances. He tasted of barley. It was fun. I ran my tongue along his teeth. Slidey and gooey. I was kissing and being kissed. I was normal. I was a teenager kissing. I could do it. I wanted to run around the town naked, yelling full blast: "HALLELUJAH, HALLELUJAH, I am a kisser, I can kiss. I'm a FRENCH KISSER!!"

When I looked in the mirror the next morning I saw with gruesome embarrassment that I had a clown's mouth—all that kissing had chafed my upper lip and doubled its parameters. At breakfast in the cafeteria, I tried to eat with one hand casually covering my mouth. Idaho said I should be careful of Toronto private school boys; they were rich and ambitious. Albertans like to make fun of eastern boys, saying their nails were clean but their motives were dirty, but I thought Johnny was supernaturally beautiful now that he had kissed me. And I liked that his excessive use of cologne drowned out the town's aluminum smell.

We spent all of the following evenings together by the river chugging Le Vigneron (three-dollar white wine) out of the bottle. He always remembered to get me a straw for the wine. We fooled around. He sucked my neck and gave me a hickey the size of Lake Ontario. I was mortified and pleased; it was a badge of honour.

During the day, we students went to class for five hours, going over and over the complications and nuances of French grammar. The teachers knew we partied and were tolerant of our daytime sleepiness. They understood that the best way to learn the language was to socialize and that eventually we would understand the whole direct and indirect object/subject agreement liaison stuff.

Johnny and I spent a lot of time liaising and eating poutine at Chez Max with our buddies. Johnny and his friends were the type of guys who made fart noises with their hands in their armpits, but they were funny enough. His friend told me Johnny got suspended from school because he mooned some family driving by when he was on the school bus going on a field trip. Johnny used words like horny when I would have said amorous.

Sex for me seemed like a faraway country I would go to some day way in the future. "What are blue balls?" I asked when he said he hated them one night, lying in my single bed. Unlike him I was happy to roll around for days, just playing together. It was like I had a chastity belt in my mind that no eighteen-year-old Houdini could crack. Both Isobel and I had no intention of losing our virginities that summer. Isobel was getting busy with Idaho, but every time he would get too steamy, she had flashing images of her mother. Still, she was a faster learner than me.

I was a little intimidated by Johnny. Boys and penises were so foreign, I didn't know how to approach them. As the summer nights rolled by, I worried. I knew Johnny was a fast mover, and there were only so many dodging routines I could maintain. I could shift to lying on my tummy. I could try to distract him with kisses. I could grab his hands and put them around my neck. I particularly liked being his girlfriend when there was no danger of sex; riding the public bus was ideal—I made him do a lot of sightseeing. I liked it when he kissed my earlobe and breathed in my ear.

One night he reached for my pants. "I think you're really special, Annie." He unzipped his fly. "I want to show you how I really feel for you. I really like you, Annie. You've got the face of a cherub girl when you come out from behind your hair."

His compliments made me feel wonderful. I felt indebted, almost obliged to give him something back, but I still knew I would not be able to go that far. We smooched, and he continued to make attempts at unzipping my pants. Each time I managed to catch his hands. I had to be vigilant. I did try to touch his penis one time, but it felt like a weird rock.

After three weeks of stiffies sans action, he said, "Look, I don't want to play anymore. It's not worth it."

"What do you mean? I thought you thought I was special? Johnny?"

"Thing is, I'm eighteen years old, and this is my summer."

"Your summer for what?"

"Never mind, Annie, I'm going to sleep in my room tonight. You should try not to be such a tease."

"What do you mean *tease*? I don't want to get pregnant, Johnny! I'm not on the pill and a girl can pregnant the first time she has sex and what would I do then? I can't get pregnant. I'm *fifteen*; I'm not on the *pill*."

"Pregnant, that's a joke! You think you can pregnant with your panties on?! Grow up, Annie!"

He walked out. I felt sick. It reminded me of the first time I ever got winded when I had fallen off a swing in the park and landed flat smack down on my back. I stayed in my room for two days with only intermittent visits from Isobel, who was mostly busy canoodling with Idaho.

I felt like it was the end of the world.

Isobel said she felt like she was in a movie. Turns out Idaho was as romanced by *A Room with a View* as we were, although he did tell us we should read the book as it was far superior. He had studied George Emmerson's mannerisms and liked to make a question mark out of the food on his plate. Isobel had no problem pretending to be Lucy Honeychurch. She had practised talking about Beethoven for months. They dressed up in linens, which tellingly they'd both packed. He coiffed his hair like George. She mock brooded and had fits of passion. They played tennis in the early evenings and drank tea. Idaho told us we had to see *Betty Blue* and *Diva*; he introduced us to French cinema, Gabriel Garcia Marquez, and all things cool. He wore trendy jeans and studied theatre. He was so sophisticated we felt almost worldly just by association.

But I wasn't feeling so glamorous when I finally left my room because for the next five days Johnny avoided me. I didn't know what to do except try not to look too woeful—it was challenging. I concentrated on looking bored. Friday night Isobel, Idaho, and I were doing the usual post-dancing eating thing at Chez Max and Johnny was there with a big group of people. I avoided looking at him and focused on my Fuzzy Navel and that strange Goth guy from Manitoba who tried to convince me that it was way colder there than in Alberta. I didn't believe him. I went downstairs to go find Isobel but saw her cornering Johnny near the bathrooms. I lurked behind the cigarette machine to watch.

"Why did you stop seeing Annie?" She asked him, mock beating his chest.

I felt sick.

I slinked back up the stairs so they wouldn't see me. I ordered a beer and sat sipping it while Reuben from Montreal tried to talk to me about banjos and "Funky Town" played on the radio for the third time that night. I hid behind my hair and tried not to cry. Two minutes later there was a banging noise coming from the stairs; instead of someone falling down the stairs it sounded like someone was falling up them. I looked at the doorway and saw Isobel with her hand in his waistband dragging Johnny up the stairs like he was on a leash. His shirt was untucked and I could see the tanned skin of his hip. When they got to the top, both laughing, she took a big breath, squatted a little, and picked him up fireman-style, over her shoulder, and brought him over to me like some sort of sacrificial offering.

"Il veut te dire quelque chose, Annie."

"Put me down, Izzy."

"Cry uncle, Johnny!"

I was totally embarrassed but a little amused too. Isobel was sweating under the exertion of carrying a one-hundred-and-eighty-pound guy over her shoulder. She did have broad shoulders and was a strong girl, but it looked like a struggle. They both collapsed on the floor in a laughing mess of arms and legs and skin. When they finally got up, he looked right at me.

"Hi, Annie." He smiled.

I nodded.

It seemed all quiet in Chez Max for a moment until, surprisingly, he sat himself right down on my lap and helped himself to a swig of my beer. The din resumed, and he leaned close and whispered in my ear, "I've missed you, my Alberta girl. Would you take me back? Please? Purrrrtyy please, lil darling?"

I felt a wave of warmth flood my chest. It drowned my indignation over being ditched and picked up again. We stayed together for the last week of the program. He seemed to accept my virginity and resigned himself to drinking beer and playing tic-tac-toe on my thighs. I wondered what had made him come back when I wasn't giving him what he wanted. I secretly hoped he really liked me, but I didn't want to spook him by asking any questions.

After we'd been back in Alberta for a couple of days, Isobel and I discovered we both had mono and glands the size of golf balls in our necks. Johnny sent a postcard saying: *I've got mono, what a drag! Too tired to write more. love, Johnny xoxoxo.* It was my first love letter and I was delighted, despite my fatigue.

Because mono was also known as the kissing disease, Mom got suspicious: "What kind of funny business were you up to in Quebec? I think maybe there was too much alcohol and mischief! Were all three of you kissing each other?"

"Mooooooommmmmm! Don't be ridiculous. We were there studying French. Studying, not partying! We barely had time to leave our desks."

"Don't exaggerate, Annie! You don't get mono in the library."

"But—"

"Don't but me. Get some sleep."

As I spent days half-sleeping on the couch, I listened to Robert Charlebois, and I thought about Quebec and wondered if that night downstairs at Chez Max, Isobel and Johnny had kissed. But the summer and everything had been so great, it didn't even really matter. We had been finally living real life. I never asked her if something had happened. No matter what, she was my pal first and foremost. Give and take was part of the sisterhood. Besides, we could have got mono from sharing Fuzzy Navels and Black Label beer. We did share everything back then.

Isobel's whole Frenchy thing started all those years ago. And now all these years later we listened to Leonard Cohen deadpan romance us through the leafy streets of small-town Quebec singing songs about girls peeling oranges. I chewed a piece of cinnamon gum and thought how I'd gone from reading *Harriet the Spy* to Mordecai Richler and yet I still felt like the same young girl. Looking in the rear-view mirror I definitely looked older. And I had a car. The car was now ridiculously dirty with hundreds of dead bugs plastered on the windscreen. Sullivan and I used to like to go to carwashes in his truck and kiss while the whole world was covered in soap and giant black and yellow bumblebees squished us in their underwater hugs.

At our next pit stop, Isobel went to get us some poutine at the dep. I headed for a phone booth.

"Finn, how are you? We miss you. I miss you."

"I miss you too, how's it goin?"

"Good, you know, we're in Quebec now."

"Ah, la belle province!"

"Do you know if the boss is going to send me an advance? Sorry to bug you . . ."

"They gave it to me, and I put it in your account for you."

"Aw, Finn, you're so great. Now we can get home."

"So, has Isobel, you know, said anything . . . ?"

"Oof . . . sorry, Finn, I think you know what . . . I think you just gotta let go of that one. She's not ready for such a great guy as you."

"Ya I know, maybe when we're in our thirties she'll have an epiphany. I'll be peaking then in charisma. How's the road trip going anyway?"

"Finn, thanks so goddamn much for the guitar! We busked,

I sang, Isobel sang. We met this crazy English dude, and we all jammed."

"That's great. I've been thinking we should start a band . . ."

"Really? I don't know . . . maybe . . . I'll talk to Isobel."

The operator cut in to tell us that I was running out of money.

"Call me again. Call collect. Any time!!"

"Salut!"

"She'll be coming round the mountain when
she comes
Singing ay, ay, yippee, yippee, ay"
Old African American Spiritual and
19th-Century American Folk Song

Day 7 continued

In Quebec for this second time I thought I'd give Izzy all my Johnnies as long as she didn't try to woo my Hawksley. My odds were slim at best, but I was scared they'd be nil if she went up to bat. I had the dim sense that now, nine years older, we were still foolish girls. But I knew Hawksley wouldn't approve of that negative line of thought—he would tell me to rely on my animal urges.

I wanted to make sure we weren't late so I insisted on driving the last leg, red eye. Isobel had wanted to park somewhere so we could get a good night's rest, but I was stubbornly against it: who needed sleep when great love was on the horizon? And so on I drove, giddy with the combination of lack of sleep and a gut feeling that no matter what, when the sun rose and the new day broke, I was going to speak to Hawksley Workman in the flesh.

No matter what the outcome—I would meet the man who made the tunes that tapped deep into my happy bone. And on and on I drove, wilfully ignoring my thinking mind and embracing my animal self.

I just needed to stay awake long enough to get us there safely. Problem was, I couldn't blast the tunes because Isobel needed to sleep. I decided to take some of her Sudafed. I wasn't congested or anything, but my brother told me he took it when he needed to stay up late to study for exams. I took two and washed them down with my cold gas station coffee that slopped in a Styrofoam cup wedged between my thighs. The car smelled stale. I opened the window a crack and enjoyed the breeze on my face. It was three o'clock in the morning and quite light out. I had the big harvest moon keeping me company. Felt like an omen. I hoped I wasn't about to get my period.

We were still two hundred-ish klicks from the lights of Montreal, thanks to some geographical noodling and bad sign reading. The highway was almost empty except for long-haul truckers, Greyhound buses, the odd car, and me. I was behind a giant beer truck. It was painted with one huge, orange wraparound ad for a classic Québécois beer called Maudite. I alternated staring at the licence plate and giant tires and the little Lucifer guy spread across the back door and the apocalyptic LA FIN DU MONDE. Gotta love how those Québécois have a beer called Damned.

My foot was committed to the gas pedal but staring endlessly at the same satanic imagery was really zoning me out. It was too easy, that was the problem with the TransCanada. There weren't so many winding turns or narrow stretches, not like the Coquihalla, where you had to be alert like Jacques Villeneuve racing along the mountainscape while wild rivers raged with white-water rapids far below.

I tried to not get psyched out like I knew I could, but once the first inkling of fear entered my head it was near impossible to stop the panic process in motion. My heart picked up its pace.

Shit . . . here we go.

I can't have an attack behind the wheel.

Oh NO. I'll crash, I'll kill us both. I visualized our blood and guts on the windscreen; imagined my head decapitated and lying beside a dead gopher—just more roadkill. I saw Isobel's eyeball impaled on the antenna. I fought not to close my eyes to escape my gore-filled visions; I had to keep my eyes focused on the giant beer truck ahead. I saw Hawksley laying a roadside wreath for me.

Calm down, calm the fuck down, I told myself. RELAX, GODDAMMIT! You're just driving. It's fine, you're just nervous. You're not panicking. You're holding the steering wheel just fine, you're driving along, it's all wonderful. Never should have taken that Sudafed! Soon you'll be in Montreal. You'll be talking to Hawksley, maybe even smooching Hawksley. Mmm. Concentrate on the road. Think Zen. Yellow lines, tail lights, and green signs. That's all you gotta do. Make sure your feet and hands stay awake. Wiggle your toes. Visualize smooching Hawksley . . . straddling Hawksley . . . eating spaghetti meatballs off Hawksley's stomach. Ooo. I wanted to lick his ribcage. I wanted him to look at me adoringly, like he couldn't believe how lucky he was, how perfect for him I was, how he wanted me more than anything. I wanted to watch sunsets with him, have Jacuzzis together, flirt like strangers, fuck like rabbits, and hold hands like otters . . .

What would I say to him? How would I captivate him and showcase all my best qualities? What were my best qualities? I was nice, funny sometimes, I had great taste in music, books, films. I had amazing friends. I had strong calves. Muscular forearms from waitressing. I knew how to French kiss underwater.

One thing I'd learned with the Bern interview, charm on demand was an oxymoron for me and spontaneous charm was a question of alchemy. The pressure might thwart me completely—give me charm impotence. What if I was obnoxious? Maybe I needed some mnemonic codes for conversation topics . . .

I psyched myself out so easily; it was my fundamental problem in life. Like the last time I was shooting stick and I tried to hit the eight ball and I got in the zone and all was quiet around me like it was supposed to be right before you hit and everything slowed down and I was ready to shoot. Then I had the stupid thought about distracting myself and I blasted that eight ball right off the table. Airborne. On bad days, I *was* Woody Allen. I couldn't shut up about my neuroses, peccadilloes. When the self-loathing bastard in my head woke up for the day I felt like that person in the painting *The Scream*. Maybe a lot of people feel like that.

Let go, Annie. Let go. This is one of those things you gotta just trust in the universe.

It was amazing how big Isobel's snores were for such a graceful girl. She sounded like a goddamned rhinoceros. Jesus. She needed to do something about her adenoids. Maybe they could be lasered out or something. I thought about sleeping.

One thing I was sure of, I didn't want to be Isobel. I was comfortable in my skin, despite the demons. They were my demons. I didn't like the look of her demons.

I had been noticing lately how she ate vicariously through me. She was always buying me food, encouraging me to have desert, but she always had an excuse why she wouldn't indulge herself. It was getting on my nerves. My jeans were getting tighter. For years I'd have burgers, and she'd have a leaf of lettuce and a Diet Coke, always saying she'd eaten at home. Now that we were on the road I was noticing more and more how she had more chewing gum than actual food. But she did drink loads of booze, diet pops, and coffee.

Maudite ahead seemed to have picked up his pace. I stepped on the gas, I couldn't risk losing him. The lorry had Montreal listed in its address and I was gambling on it being my guide into town.

I thought of this movie where this beautiful brunette girl approached a stubbly strange man in a bar. His novel had rocked her gypsy soul, so she followed/stalked him and then pitched her love to him in a café one night. He was so touched by her bravery that he fell in love with her on the spot and they went off to celebrate and have sex that same night. Surely it could happen for me just like that. It seemed realistic in the movie.

Wasn't Priscilla just a big Elvis fan at the start too? And I think I read Paula Yates was a girl just hanging around the music scene when she hooked up with Bob Geldof. And that was in real life, not just in the movies. I bet there are countless unions between fans and stars. I wondered how groupies shook off their groupie status and became bona fide girlfriends.

Someone told me every author needed only one perfect reader. Every singer surely needed one true listener. I was his listener. I understood his lyrics; I lived them. His lyrics were true and, like sexy Keats said, "Beauty is truth, truth beauty."

Checking the rear-view mirror to look at the state of my hair, I saw a guy in the car behind us wearing some kind of funny hat, not quite a cowboy hat, a cross between cowboy and sombrero? Weirdly I was almost sure that I'd been seeing him at night, every night on the road. But not during the day.

My first thought was that it was Finn in disguise.

My second thought was that it was an agent from my VISA credit card company come to throw me in debtors jail.

My third thought was that it was road-trip déjà vu.

He was nondescript and so was his car. His hat was a little unusual, but angles and shadows were surely doing their bit to distort my view.

I looked at the speedometer. I stared at it until it made no sense. I didn't look in the mirror again.

After more and more and more and more kilometres of staring at the LA FIN DU MONDE banner ahead and the yellow highway lines passing underneath us, Isobel's three-octave snore calmed me and diffused my paranoia. I was just a bit jittery still. It was getting lighter outside too. I had another gulp of cold coffee. I think the Sudafed was kicking in and making my eyes feel more open. My heart felt like it was part of a Latin percussion ensemble. I stretched my fingers on the wheel and tried to sit up straight, working on my breathing and my game plan.

Day 8 Dawn
4,541 kms!!!

We pulled into Montreal at dawn. I felt like I'd been assaulted by the challenge. The only way I managed to get us through the clusterfuck of terrifying overpasses and bridges and confusing signs coming into Sin City was because Maudite's driver was indeed going into town too. Guardian Angels come in funny disguises. My heavy eyelids had long ago lost sight of the Man with the Strange Hat's car. It was 5:00 AM, and the big fat orange sun was rising in its full glory on the quiet but funky streets of downtown. We were too early for bagels, too early for coffee, but perfect for flower raiding. I felt funny. A bit dizzy, almost seasick. Izzy woke up grumpy, dehydrated, and badly needing to pee.

I stopped at a gas station. I loved seeing French signs for everything, French people everywhere. Getting out of the car we must have looked like arthritic oldies, all gimped up from sitting in the same position for six hours. We snuck into the bathroom and tried to clean ourselves without touching any of the grim-looking surfaces.

"This is totallement dégoutant! Cochons pissing all over the floor. And let me tell you, it's a special kind of imbécile that wets toilet paper and hucks it at the ceiling. Don't these cochons ever think about the poor people who clean these places, and they're usually immigrants, it's terrible!" Ever since we'd crossed the border Isobel had ramped up her Franglais.

"You could fill out the customer complaint card. C'mon, let's just get out of here and find some coffee and bagels and a park to sit in." I wanted to protect the mood of the day. It had to be right. Not tense.

"Oui!" said Isobel.

The downtown streets were empty. We parked the car and walked around looking for a place to hang out until we stumbled onto the grounds of McGill and parked ourselves under a giant cedar tree until it was coffee time. We figured nothing would open until at least 8:00 AM. It was heaven being out of the car and in the fresh air.

After a good rest, we got back in the car and somehow navigated our way over to Fairmont Street to pick up some bagels. We had never forgotten the sublimeness of proper Montreal bagels when we tried them all those years ago. The bagel makers were up early shovelling the glistening white dough with their long spoons into the dark womb of the huge, crackling wood-burning oven. Isobel reckoned we should get a bag of twenty-four because they were so goddamned delicious. They could be our sustenance for the whole way home. The difference between these lovely skinny and airy Montreal bagels and the rest of Canada's doughier ones is that you can taste water in these ones. According to some random guy at the store it had something to do with boiling them and baking them at sea level.

We drove over to a coffee shop on St. Urbain, the street I'd read about in Mordecai Richler's longwinded but gut-bustingly funny novels. The view now before me was so exotic for my Albertan eyes: the two-storey red and brown brick apartment suites with their long staircases down to the front path, like big inviting tongues. Sure we had the odd old building in Alberta; they called them character apartments, but they were freaks and were mostly being knocked down. This was like the Europe of my imagination—or even better, a fabulous fusion of old and new worlds.

The owners of the coffee shop were old-school Italian men in their late sixties. There were soccer posters on the wall, Italian flags and photos of famous Italians: Pacino, Sophia Loren, Pavarotti. Before I could order anything, the elder man behind the counter sized me up and instructed the guy on the chrome espresso machine beside him: Cappuccino. The machine was regal-looking, with a silver eagle perched on top, extending its full wingspan.

Gramps looked at Isobel and said: Espresso, double. He had a white, short-sleeved shirt on with a blue-and-white tea-towel swung cavalierly over his shoulder. I think every major town in Canada had the same version of this kind of bare bones Italian coffee shop. I'd been to one in Vancouver on

Commercial Drive, Joe's, the little pool hall with velour wall hangings of matadors and elderly cappuccino makers. E-town had one over in Little Italy where Isobel and I sometimes went to scope all those Euro-hotties.

We found ourselves a nice spot on the patio and sat down with our coffees. It was prime people-watching territory. My cappuccino was gorgeous. Not too much milk, just a creamy, slightly stiff cloud of foam on top and a strong dose of espresso. This was the kind of coffee that tasted just as good as freshly ground beans smell. Out of three hundred and sixty-five cups in a year, you might remember less than a handful—this one was in the top three.

To bagel purists, it might have seemed like sacrilege, but I went all the way and slathered a bagel with cream cheese and blackcurrant jam that we'd also bought in little tubs. Then I dunked the bagel in my coffee. Bliss, happiness. I could feel Isobel watching me. She picked at her bagel in between puffs of her cigarette. She shot back her espresso and went to order another. By this point in our road trip, we weren't speaking much; we'd run out of topics.

I watched the other customers. I was so attracted to Montrealers; they were a sexy bunch. It's not that they dressed fancy, they just seemed to have a just-rolled-out-of-bed innate chic. Our classic Albertan men with their baseball caps and Oilers sweatshirts couldn't compete romantically with the Québécois men in their loose blazers and woolly turtleneck insouciance. Theirs was a nonchalant elegance. Not pretentious, just distilled Euro flair. Think Leonard Cohen. Plus they had that whole bilingual thing happening; they could woo in French *and* English.

Isobel came walking back over to the table with a latte. She looked a bit like a flapper with her sleeveless, jade green short dress and her Cleopatra haircut. "The old man thought two double espresso back to back wouldn't be idéale."

The morning got hotter and hotter as we sat there sipping coffee and eating bagels, reading newspapers until lunchtime. By noon it felt like +40 and humid. Steam-room humid. I took some more cold medicine. I was surprisingly alert for having not slept yet.

We took off down Mont-Royal East, needing to find a flower shop or a well-stocked flowerbed in a public park. It was imperative that I found a red flower so Hawksley would be able to recognize my signal like I'd told him in my letter. After milling up and down the streets for a while, and seeing no flower shops, Isobel pointed at a flower box in someone's front yard. A whole box of red snapdragons. I looked in the windows, saw no one, and so bent down and struggled to break off one from the bunch. I had to shimmy it from side to side and then yank it out from the root.

I wasn't sure how good it would look in my hair, this snapdragon with its puffy petals that looked like painted earlobes on a stalk. I felt shame for stealing it and leaving a flower tomb in the soil. A flower robber. "Come on, Annie, we're going to be late, what are you doing? Why are you sticking a bagel in the dirt? Those bagels are precious, Annie, Montreal bagels, for heaven's sakes." The bagel felt like the right thing to fill the gap. Maybe the flower bed owners would understand the swap.

Isobel helped to secure the flower properly in my ponytail's elastic band. She said it looked a bit like I was wearing an Indian headdress, but not to worry Indian chic was all the rage. I had been aiming more for flamenco dancer.

When we got back out on the street we saw it was much more crowded. Downtown Montreal and the streets were now heaving. People of all ages strolled everywhere. I wondered if there was a parade or some kind of protest. It was mad. People were barely clothed. So much flesh. God I loved summer!

Summery people in their light clothes, all just sliding along in rivers of summer sweat. We joined the crowd and walked for a block. I hoped we could get off the main road, but when I looked down the other street, it was packed, feeding onto Saint-Laurent. I felt nervous in the crowds, claustrophobic. I hadn't experienced a heat wave in forever. My heart pounded; I was definitely overheating.

Unlike me, Isobel could see over most people's heads. "I could lift you up on my shoulders, if you're feeling claustrophobic." The fact that she knew me so well mellowed my mounting fear. We considered slithering across the car roofs to get to the gig on time. I stood up on a bumper of an old Citroën to see ahead. All I could see were swarms of more people.

And then it hit me.

Everyone was headed to the mountain that day for the free concert.

They were all headed for my Hawksley.

We were but two in a sprawling, buzzing mob.

He had become, without my noticing, a megastar, no longer an indie fave with a cult following; the masses were involved. My stomach forecasted doom.

When we got to the mountain area, we saw an outdoor stage. I did a double take. Hawksley was walking on stage! It was too early, surely. No, it was Him. But it didn't look like we could get anywhere near the stage. I felt sick realizing I'd driven red-eyed to get to the city early and somehow, lost in coffee land, I had messed up and now we were late. My eyes welled up. My nose felt stuffed. I felt Isobel looking at me. Isobel rose to the challenge. "Don't worry, darling. I'll get you to him, ma chérie!" She grabbed my hand and shimmied us through the crowd, "Excuse me, excusé moi, merci, nous sommes Albertaines!" and wandangled us to the front. At one point she even hoisted me onto people's arms. I was crowd surfing, which would normally have deeply embarrassed me, but here I was an anonymous Albertan. It was just a little ticklish.

Hawksley was alone on stage, without his disciples, the Wolves. He cleared his throat. With Isobel beside me, now up close to the stage, I waited anxiously, my heart pounding. Sick with anticipation. He closed his eyes and looked like he was meditating. My salivary glands spurted as if there was a chocolate eclair within my reach. I wiped the sweat off my forehead and worried about my blood pressure dropping.

"Salut, Montréal! Ça va? Ça trippe? Ça gaze? Eh oui, j'espère que toute la gang icite se sent fort fort sexy aujourd'hui! J'en ai ben des chansons là pour vous autres, si vous en désirez?"

The crowd roared and clapped and wolf-whistled. The grass was lovely and green, the sky was blue, the woods were full of bouncing life. Summer, Montreal-style, hot and sweaty.

He was wearing a fetching, episcopal purple blousy shirt underneath a suit vest and he had on matching pinstriped trousers—vintage shop chic. From a distance, it looked like he had safety-pinned his fly together; I was intrigued. I admired his sideburns and roguish black curly hair. His beauty was frightening, almost too much for me to bear.

He opened with "Bullets," which he spiced up with a four-minute tap-dance solo that made the crowd swoon. While he tapped away, he held an angelic high note and kept us all in breathless rapture.

Following his spectacular opening feats, a girl in the audience with pigtail braids, who was balanced on top of a guy wearing a vintage military green jacket, pitched a handful of flowers on stage: blue, purple, red, yellow, and orange African daisies. He bent down to pick them up one by one and blew the girl a kiss.

He gathered the daisies together, arranging them into a bouquet, and then held it with both hands and pretended he was holding a bat. He swung them luxuriously in the air, hitting an invisible baseball. It was beautiful. So beautiful that the cynical thought crossed my mind that he'd arranged for the girl to give him the flowers; it was hard to imagine he could improvise such poetic elegance.

But I dismissed the thought pretty quickly; the man was an Artist.

He rested his arms over his left shoulder, daisies dangling, and sang a vaudevillian number about a man named Johnny.

He then ripped off a few petals and ate them.

Stopped to put on some lipstick.

Sang a song about stripping for your lover while he licked out sharp 1970s electric guitar riffs.

The crowd went nuts.

I could see his tonsils wiggle.

I felt hot.

The crowd pogoed up and down.

As always, his shtick brought everyone together, like we were in on the joke. Everyone around me was fanning themselves. Couples danced lewdly. His spooky aphrodisiac effect had kicked in: girls smiled, purring like cats; boys puffed out their chests like peacocks. Winks and bashful nods. These uninhibited Québécois made it feel like one big summer festive mating dance.

A man beside me turned to me and said, "I've got the shivers."

I nodded knowingly.

Hawksley was a joy peddler, a love promoter, a bliss manufacturer. I could feel the endorphins releasing wave after wave in my brain, my mood elevating, my spirit soaring, my libido roaring. Love for everyone and everything, compassion, forgiveness. Serotonin was dancing in my brain. I had the feeling of pride when I saw him play, even felt a surging of corny patriotism: Canada produced this guy, we could hold our heads high as a nation.

Isobel turned to me and yelled, "YOU'RE RIGHT, HE'S SO MUCH MORE DIVINE LIVE."

"I KNOW, HE'S SO HOT-BLOODED!" I screeched just as the music died down. Hot-blooded and Poetic.

He let out a moan, the kind you might do when your toes are curling from your lover's caresses. The crowd hollered.

He moaned again.

The crowd cheered.

He shook his hips Elvis-style.

The crowd whistled.

A girl on Isobel's left kept repeating, "Fabulous. Fabulous. Fabulous . . ."

He moaned himself into a frenzy, playing his guitar like he was in love with it. He threw himself down on the ground. A fan jumped up on stage and mopped his brow.

I almost forget from gig to gig how goddamned gorgeous he was. How over-the-top sexy he was. How he flirted, lamented, crooned, and seduced. My arm hairs stood up, like a strong breeze had blown them. My smile was hurting my face it was so intense.

I could see that I wasn't the only one smiling, the whole crowd was high, girls and boys.

Business owners on the streets opposite the park were out in front of their restaurants, corner shops. People on balconies in high-rises waved and clapped. In the distance, I saw a deer coming to the edge of the woods. Were there even squirrels standing to attention? Could have been Sudafed hallucinations.

We were all enamoured with Hawksley's lust for life. His every yip revved up the crowd. He flattered. He flirted. He made fun of himself. He played matador, teasing an imaginary bull with a faux-fur red coat that he pulled out of a costume trunk on stage.

Between songs, he drank tea from a pottery mug. He said he liked it with lots of honey, like his grandma used to make for him. He spoke of his grandparents between songs, retuning his guitar. "My grandpa was a farmer, he, like, loved birds . . . you know what I'm saying? This one year the drought was so bad, he couldn't sleep at night 'cause he worried about the birds not being able to make nests 'cause it was so dry there was, like, no mud. None. So I go to visit him, right, and he'd be there—watering a patch of dirt. And I'd say, 'What are you doing, Grandpa?' And he'd say, 'Just making the birds some mud.' Every day for the whole drought he'd water that patch. You can see why Grandma was crazy in love with him . . . Now Grandma . . . she taught me how to put on lipstick and play poker. I love visiting them . . . They're in a different lane than everyone else . . . you know what I mean?" When he was done tuning and talking he launched into "Striptease," an anthem call for primal sex.

"So did you guys all see the full moon last night? I mean WOW, I don't know about you, but I felt a bit hairy. I started scratching and sniffing and, man, pretty soon I was a werewolf. I sat on that little balcony and did some howling, because . . . well . . . it felt good! I think us humans are too caught up in our minds, we need to get back to our bodies, back to our animal desires. You know what I'm saying?"

The crowd cheered and barked and howled and honked up at him.

"And you know for some weird reason the moon makes me think about Christmas . . . you know, in that kind of holy way that I think we should see more of all year-round. So in between howling at the moon, I sang a song, maybe you know it . . ."

With no other instruments he started singing "Silent Night." It was so surprising, like eating strawberries with ground pepper. And so even though it was a super-humid August summer afternoon with a blue sky and green grass, the crowd joined in.

It didn't feel odd or wrong to be earnestly singing "Silent Night," it felt wonderful.

By the final chorus, I opened my eyes and felt sick with love for him. It was almost too much pleasure. I couldn't go outside to get some air, this was outside. But I knew I wasn't going to pass out this time—I was beyond that.

Isobel turned to me, wiping the sweat from her brow, still singing, "Ho-oh-ly Night, Si-eye-lent Night, All is calm, all is bright . . ." Once she realized that everyone else had stopped singing, she stopped and said, "Wow!"

Behind her then I saw something that jolted me out of ecstasy. I caught sight of the Guy from the Rear-view Mirror.

Was he wearing a red jacket? In this heat? He had no hat. Why did I think he was the same guy?

I dismissed the paranoia by switching channels in my brain and visualizing Finn. I wondered how he was doing. I wished he was here for our impending rock-star encounter Number 3. After Hawksley graciously and deliciously played five encores, the crowd reluctantly let him go, only because he was sounding a bit hoarse.

It was time to go backstage.

Finn had doctored our media passes from the Bern caper so we would be able to have access to the green room. Except there was a lineup as long as the North Saskatchewan and it serpentined forever through the park. An infinite tail of girls and women from early teens to the seniors. Big ones, little ones, spiky-haired, curly-haired, big-hatted, small-skirted, tight-T-shirted, boob-tubed, gum-snapping, perfume-wearing, eyelash-batting women! All of them were flushed and had that just-got-Hawksleyed look. And they were meandering all the way from the stage to the St. Lawrence. The seagulls were hovering above the queue, like they were lined up as well.

The disturbing thing was, when I looked closely, it looked like several of these women had media passes just like ours. I could make out bits of plastic in their hands and T-shirts with newspaper logos on them. Low-down, stinking Liars, all of them. And their faces, their blushing red faces. We were all interlopers.

I had allowed myself to forget how ridiculous a mission this was. How being a fan among thousands is unpleasant. How degrading it was to realize I really was just one in a desperately long line of Hawksley-eyed gaga women. I looked them up and down. I couldn't possibly muster enough superiority to rise above them all. He belonged to all of us.

I knew I had allowed myself to get wooed. Wowed and wooed. But I don't know when exactly I got reckless and pelted myself across the line from normal listener to girl chasing boy. Willingly letting myself fantasize about Hawksley and me together, of the possibilities. Once I was on the other side, there was no going back. Being delusional was enjoyable. He was a love evangelist, and I was converted. I had given up on love after Sullivan, and Hawksley had saved my soul.

I watched them fanning themselves. I felt like throwing up as we waited in line. I looked at the sky and concentrated on cloud-sculpting. My epic delusion was revealing itself to me, I could now imagine an advertising blimp trailing a banner across the sky in upper caps: GIVE IT UP, LET IT GO, HE'S JUST A ROCK STAR, YOU'RE JUST A FAN. He would never be mine alone. It was wrong to try to hoard him. But I didn't even like sharing him with Isobel, let alone all of these strangers.

But we were finally here, so I had to go through with it, for the sake of resolution. I needed closure, goddammit.

My stomach was all nerves, still jumbling and rumbling, and my heart was still pounding too fast. I ignored the chorus in my head saying, WALK AWAY, LET GO. There were only thirty more women ahead of us in the lineup to speak to him.

Two hours later, and with hope now in the minus department, I felt like we were all a herd of baby turtles making our way to the big sea trying to avoid being attacked by birds knowing that once we arrived, any number of predators could drown us. The line was barely advancing. I was worried about heat stroke, and Isobel was worried about lipstick melting. I was grateful she hadn't run out of patience. Our media pass hadn't helped at all.

The whole set up wasn't how I'd imagined it would be. I wasn't going to be spending the night with Hawksley somewhere. I wasn't going to entertain him with my funniest jokes, perform my entire repertoire of good stories, or impress him with how wild and charming I was. He wouldn't care that I was his biggest listener, how I was the one for him. He wasn't going to fall madly in love with me. The more I looked at the other women, I saw that they were fans in love with his Hawksleyness, just like I was.

Tears streamed down my face. A girl beside me said, "He's going to love your panda eyes, darling." Her friend, who was also crying, told her to shut up.

I didn't want to share him anymore with these crazy chicks, but I felt my motivation already leaving me, saying, See you later, cowgirl. I was going through the motions, but I knew I would just keep doing that because there'd been too many kilometres; Alberta was too far a place to come from to stop now. Like when I was with Sullivan, a part of me needed the humiliation of rejection to truly put my obsession back in perspective, maybe even squash it forever. I drummed up the last of my delusion to fire myself up—I pictured kissing him in a bubble bath.

I stared at the backs of two heads in front of me. I couldn't hear what they were saying, but Hawksley was laughing and they were swaying. Sounded like one of them was reciting a poem. Talented cows! How was I going to vie for his attention?

The girls ahead of us said their goodbyes and smiled smugly at us as they walked dreamily away. Isobel lunged forward. I felt venom rising up in me as I watched her arch her back coquettishly and purse her lips in that new way she'd been developing lately à la French actrice (like a slow-mo pout).

I hadn't said a word, and she was already chatting him up in her strange-bordering-on-offensive way: "Can you believe all this?!" she said, gesturing to the crowd of people surrounding him and the lineup, including me. "I mean, what's the fuss all about—it's just *you!*" she said laughingly like they were old friends. It was classic Isobel behaviour; she resented anyone else's fame.

But she went too far when she had leaned toward him, offering her hand like a princess for him to kiss. She was taking over. She didn't possess the grace to not be the centre of attention for once.

I decided violence was the way forward.

With as much subtlety as possible, I put a big smile on my face and simultaneously crashed down on Isobel's cranberry-painted toes. It was my most assertive act ever. Izzy stifled a screech and backed away gracefully, understanding the code.

At last, there he was . . . in front of me . . . alone in all his curly-haired glory.

He looked strangely smaller, subdued, and tired; this was him offstage. But he was so familiar to me. I ran through all the things I wanted to say to him in my head, how I loved him madly, how in "You Me and the Weather" I know exactly what he meant, how we could have a great time together, how . . . But what could I say that was any different from the fifteen hundred girls behind me?

"Is, is, is that episcopal purple you're wearing?"

He leaned forward and giggle-whispered, "Actually, I think it's more of a penis purple."

Oof—I didn't know how to respond to penis talk! I didn't have anything rehearsed so I did the only thing that came to mind.

I got down on one knee, and, offering him a bagel (which was the only thing in my bag resembling a ring), I said: "Hawksley Workman, you don't know me yet, but I've got a confession to make. I feel that you would soon realize how I am your listener, the one who gets everything you are saying . . . This obviously isn't the time to get into it. But do you think you might like to marry me?"

He laughed.

A gorgeous, kind laugh that ended with a smile. It warmed my heart and deflated the whole situation. He cleared his throat and said, "Oh, honeysuckle, that's a charming offer . . . Come here . . . I need to tell you a secret."

I crawled over and leaned close to him. He smelled like leather, sweat, and honey.

"I'm pretty much very married already and I'm mad about her. I'm sorry," he said as he kissed my cheek. I got to my feet. Then he gestured to come closer again. I approached. As I leaned toward him for the second time, it dawned on me: he looked a hell of a lot like Sullivan. The hair, the sultry eyes, the full lips. Weird that I hadn't noticed that before.

"Nice snapdragon!" he said to me, winking.

I walked away with Isobel limping along beside me. She threw her arm around me in solidarity. "Chin up, mon p'tit coeur.

You might not think so right now, but that was a magnifique thing you just did there. And the bagel thing, pure brilliance! No one would have guessed what you said to him."

"Come on, that was the most teeny-boppy thing I've ever done, Iz. This beats it all. I was crawling, for fucksakes . . ." I pulled out the snapdragon from my hair.

"No, trust me on this. You were very brave. You took a risk you knew would probably result in a crash and you went for it! Besides, he's not that cute close up. He kind of looks like Sullivan. Did you notice his bald patch?"

"It's hardly a bald patch, just a mild thinning in the clearing. How are your toes?"

"Let's not speak of it. It's a shame you wear those clunky boots, not just from a fashion perspective, the stomp factor is high—sweet Jesus!"

"Sorry." I didn't feel *that* sorry.

"Shush! Now let's go shopping at the merch table. A nice concert T-shirt might make it all better."

We made our way past the still-long line of girls anticipating their Hawksley blessings. I think Isobel knew she'd been offside when she'd quasi-flirted with Hawksley, so she wasn't angry about my toe-stomping outburst. But when I noticed the blood creeping up her toe I felt bad.

"Isobel, stop walking, we need to fix that."

"Mon Dieu, it's bleeding! It's fine, I'm fine, I'll rest it in the car. We'll get a little ice and it'll be healed tout de suite." She gimped along cheerfully.

The guilt added to my general feeling of self-loathing. I needed redemption. I wanted to go home and sleep for a week and then get up and start again, put it all behind me. There was no more anticipation left to fire me up, just thousands of kilometres west to be travelled.

We stopped at the merch table. Previously I'd always avoided these tables, somehow feeling holier-than-thou and not wanting regular fan merchandise because I was much much more than a fan. Those pretensions were long gone.

I fondled the T-shirts and CDs and book of poems that I already owned and then I stumbled on a miniature Hawksley statue with a bit on the bottom that you could peel off and stick to the dashboard of your car! I grabbed two, one for my mantelpiece at home. It was liberating not being proud and too good for this stuff.

Choosing stuff at the table made me think of choosing in general and how I chose this infatuation. I chose to use delusion to get over Sullivan. And my fan worship wasn't much different than my love worship I'd felt for Sullivan.

Isobel chose a pair of thong panties, which she could wear because she was tall and skinny. I tried not to think of it as blasphemy; Hawksley on her crotch. Then I saw a shadow on the table of a giant fried-egg shape. I turned around.

In full bright red Royal Canadian Mountain Police regalia stood a determined and boiling-looking man. THE GUY FROM THE REAR-VIEW MIRROR!

Oh crap, now we were going to get arrested.

"Young ladies, do you own a pink-coloured Volkswagen Beetle?"

"Uh . . . maybe," I said, imagining horrible fines for the foul fumes it had emitted across the country or for parking badly in Montreal, or maybe we'd trashed our hotel room more than I realized back in Wawa, or, worst-case scenario, for hitting something and not realizing it? Or maybe VISA had called him?

"Take me, officer. Annie has a future, she got much better marks in university than me and is super kind and has great potential as a future singer/songwriter guitarist or DJ! Take me to jail if you have to, let her go free!" I was touched by Isobel's sincerity. DJ, could I be a DJ?

"Hey, take it easy, I'm not a real RCMP! I'm wearing a bow tie! You guys must have watched way too much *Due South*; I'm just a singer in a band who dress like Mounties. RCMP don't actually dress like this on regular duty. You've maybe seen a few of us around? I was on the highway too and saw you girls a couple of times."

"Officer, I have a minor toe injury," Isobel said as she lifted her tanned leg up for him to see the wound. I think she might have flashed him a bit of panty and a whole lot of thigh. Bless her.

"Oh crumbs, that looks terrible! How'd it happen?"

"Well, c'est ridicule, but I actually stepped on myself, moi même. It's these high heels!"

"You know, you don't even need to wear high heels, miss. I mean, gosh, you're very tall as it is. You might intimidate people if you tower over their heads. I bet if I didn't have this hat on, I'd even be shorter than you."

I couldn't believe it, even this quaint RCMP guy was falling for her! It never ended. Surely the guy could see through the ditzy chick routine? Maybe he didn't *want* to see through it.

He took us to his car where he had a first-aid kit. He had her drape her leg over the seat so he could clean and dress her wound. He also managed, she told me later, to give her a sneaky little foot rub.

"Bye bye, officer!" Isobel said as we walked away.

"You know, I've never dated a cop before!"

"Isobel, come on, don't be obscene. Let's Get Pimmed!"

It was time for a Pimm's session. We were going to stay overnight at a hostel. Drinking myself to oblivion on a funny old-fashioned English drink loaded with a bunch of cucumbers and fruit was my plan.

"Terrified of telephones and shopping malls,
and knives,
and drowning in the pools of other lives.
Rely a bit too heavily on alcohol and irony.
Get clobbered on by courtesy,
in love with love,
and lousy poetry.
And I'm leaning on a broken fence
between Past and Present tense . . ."

"Aside," The Weakerthans

Day 9
Somewhere on the TransCan headed back west

I felt lower than a snake's belly, and we had almost five thousand kilometres to go before I could collapse on my couch, where I planned on spending the rest of my twenties as a failed romantic. The smell of gasoline and exhaust was blowing in through the back window, nauseating me, but it was too hot to have the window shut.

I was tired. Sleep was the only interesting thing left. And so I gave in to it, I surrendered under the weight of it. Cramped on the backseat, I felt resoundingly purposeless. I couldn't even make this whole quest funny. I couldn't hear myself retelling it—like I did with most of my debacles—it was too embarrassing.

I was having problems motivating myself to sit up, to open my eyes. My foot itched, but it seemed like too far away to scratch. My body was on strike. My head was roaring with a loud drone that drowned out even the oncoming traffic. My appetite was gone. Light hurt my eyes. My body ached from sleeping any which way. Any energy I had left, I used to preserve sleep mode. I felt guilt over Isobel doing all the driving, especially with her gimpy foot, but my guilt was buried under the obese weights of lethargy and apathy.

The next time I tried to wake up, I failed again. I didn't know what town we were in, what province, or how Isobel could drive all this time by herself. I worried I had become narcoleptic. Another affliction for the list. I couldn't think of anything to look forward to, except my couch. The present was only about shuffling from one area of discomfort to another.

By nightfall, I couldn't stay in sleep mode any longer, unless I wanted to pee myself. But I was so drugged by Morpheus that I confused vinyl with porcelain.

The wet woke me up.

I sat up quickly and got a head-rush that made me gasp. I hadn't wet myself since kindergarten. My left jean leg was soaked down the back.

"Hey, Annie, you're up! How are you?"

"I just spilled my water, all over my lap, down my pants. Jesus, what a klutz I am! Do you mind stopping at the next nice gas station so I can change everything?" Hoping desperately she wouldn't smell anything.

"Do you have any water left?"

"No, sorry, it's all on my leg!" I worried a bit because I didn't have a bottle as evidence.

"I could use a stretch myself. I think there might be a Husky coming up."

It was annoying having one leg wet and sticky. I feared the

car would start smelling; I cranked the window open wider. But as the road kept passing by and I got used to the feeling of a wet leg, I started to think that maybe it didn't matter after all. Maybe I could just keep on sleeping. Isobel hummed along to Elvis Costello.

Eventually we stopped at a Tim Hortons. Isobel went to pick a selection of doughnut holes, a twenty-five pack, and a coffee, double double. I took my spare jeans to the toilet and awkwardly did a mock shower in the sink. I dried myself off with the scratchy paper towels and put fresh jeans on. The peed-on pair I stuffed in the garbage can. Under the fluorescent lights I took a long look in the mirror. I looked like someone headed for the undertakers; plastic-bag white skin, sunken eyes, grey lips. I had puffy eyelids, car upholstery impressions on my cheek. I confirmed also that there was a boil growing to the left of my nose, just under the surface. It throbbed. Soon Mount Vesuvius would appear on my face. I didn't even bother putting on lipstick.

Hangovers are one thing, but road-trip hangovers coupled with depression and an attack of the uglies are lethal. I probably took too many Tylenols the night before, so now my heart was palpitating and my mouth was pasty and my internal organs were seasick.

The only truly good thing about the heaviness of depression was that I was almost too lethargic to be panicked. Which was kind of relaxing. We got back in the car. It looked like Isobel was chain-eating the mini-doughnuts. She had a white powder moustache, some chocolate sprinkles on her cheek, and a smile on her face. As I had freakishly lost my incredible appetite, she seemed to have gained a huge sudden gusto for food.

"Next hitchhiker we see, we grab if they have a licence, Iz."

"Why?"

"I don't feel up for driving. Think I might have the flu. We need a hand."

Isobel looked at me like I was scary, which made me feel scared for me. A new person would help the dynamic. I could feel bleakness taking me away. What was I doing with my life? My forehead felt heavy. Isobel put Elvis C. back on, I asked her to turn it off; it hurt the boil.

"You have never asked me for no music before, the whole time we've been friends. Ça va?"

"Ya, I'm just real tired. Don't worry." I was worried plenty for both of us.

The dark thoughts blew around like a whirlwind of autumn leaves caught in a windstorm in a dead-end alley. I fixated on the idea that without Iz, I was alone. I had my parents and my loved ones, but ultimately I was alone, with no purpose. The last thing I saw before I fell back asleep was some man driving beside us in a black BMW with one hand on the wheel and an index finger planted up his nose. Picking away and staring at the tarmac ahead.

I heard voices as I woke up in Ontario somewhere. I didn't know if we'd stopped for the night or just kept going. Groggy-eyed, needing to pee again and scared to have another accident, I sluggishly opened my eyes. The effort of it all made me more miserable. I looked out the window and begrudgingly admired the rolling hills and valleys. I had a prairie person's envy of hills. I came out of my fog to realize there was a new person in the driver's seat. He had a red bandanna on his head, tied pirate-style, and lots of big wooden beads around his neck. I rubbed my eyes and fought the urge to just keep sleeping and avoid having to make small talk.

"Hey, Annie, how do you like him so far? I found him at a 7-Eleven Slurpee machine in the middle of the night just outside of Sault Ste. Marie. Do you want some orange Slurpee? I got it for you."

He threw one arm behind to shake my hand. "I'm Jack. How's it going?"

I shook his hand and took the Slurpee Iz passed back. I liked his blue eyes. He was tanned, relaxed. He was our age or maybe a couple of years older. He had a rainbow-coloured tie-dyed T-shirt on and green shorts. He was a hippie; he had yin and yang earrings. He said he was from Edmonton originally but was living in Vancouver. He offered me a barley, tofu, and corn concoction from a Tupperware container in his pack, so very West-Coasty. The Slurpee was lovely and refreshing.

"So . . . um . . . I hope you're not like . . . the OTHERS!" Jack joked, with his eyes deliberately bugged way out for dramatic effect.

He spoke our language! He was quoting *Fear and Loathing*; he was an instant friend. And now that I'd determined we were safe with him, I didn't mean to be unsocial, but I felt another nap coming on. Sleep was my mercy. I closed my eyes again and tried a new neck position for the next session—I really didn't need another neck kink. Luckily the bladder alert had been a false alarm. And maybe if I kept sleeping the boil would recede.

"Is she ill or something? How much sleep does she need?" I vaguely heard Jack asking Isobel.

"She's got some serious malaise, you know how it goes . . . Things are not going so well right now, and sleep is her drug."

I was annoyed that she was giving me away. But I knew I probably would have told him myself. I was rolling into dreamland anyway. The last thing I heard was Jack saying, "I know just what she needs. A good hut. To detox her spirit."

"Are you some kind of medicine doctor?" Isobel flirted.

"No, I'm serious. I can see in her eyes, she needs some healing." He had a raspy voice. Like dry firewood.

She was a good judge of hitchhikers, that Isobel.

I woke up again and it was evening, I wondered if we were in Manitoba because Neil Young was playing again. Jack was driving, and Isobel was explaining to Jack why *The Unbearable Lightness of Being* was a seminal film: "It positively reinvigorated the stocking industry. Women all over the world, and men, realized the garter belt must come back in vogue. And don't forget what it did for the bowler hat haberdasheries!"

"Where are we?"

"Near Kenora, do you remember Kenora? We're thinking of trying to find a camping spot near a lake. Jack's got a plan for your recovery."

"What's that? What recovery, I'm fine . . . I'm just catching up on sleep from that night I missed." It was annoying being a perpetual victim, even if I cultivated it myself. It made me cranky having her always superior.

"What you need is some water therapy. Some steam to liven up your senses," said Jack.

"Like a hut?" I said.

"Ya, that's right. Wait a minute . . . you're not from that tribe of E-towners who get naked in winter and climb into saunas in your backyard?" Jack asked.

"Do you know Steamhouse Joe?"

"Of course, how 'bout Hot Stone Harry?"

"Uh huh."

We figured out the many ways our circles collided. He probably had met Sullivan too, but I didn't bring it up. I liked Jack's energy. He came across like a plain, good-time guy. Sure enough when it was his turn to pick the tunes, he rifled through my cassettes and pulled out Marley's *Legend*.

Isobel handed me some Ringolos, our last pack. I put one of each of my fingers and chomped away, feeling a bit lighter, a bit less weighted by the black dog. The familiar reggae bass soothed me. My appetite was coming back. I knew it was bad news that a guy's attention could trigger an upswing, but at that point anything that could poke a hole in the fog was a mercy.

We stopped for some supplies, then found a campsite at a place called Raven's Creek. Jack made a good strong fire, and we all drank some beers. We decided against hut that night because of our late start. By the end of the evening, Isobel had gone to bed, but I was so comfortable with Jack that I was telling him my problems. He was giving me one of the best foot rubs of my life.

"You're just going through one of those times in life, floating a bit between old wounds and new fears and that existential shit we all get lost in at some point. When you wonder what the hell is the point. We're born alone, we die alone. And we've got this life, and what the heck do we do with it, man? I know, Annie, I know . . ."

Jack had smoked a little weed at this point and was babbling, but we were mostly on the same page.

"You know what you need. Your own holy grail. There are no short cuts. You don't need to be chasing rock stars, piggyback riding on their grail . . . You need to be your own rock star.

"I'm speaking figuratively, if you know what I mean . . . using rock-starness as a general catch-all," he explained as he worked away on my feet. "You've got great feet, by the way . . . you definitely need to do some yoga . . . Yoga is the answer to every question . . ."

He rubbed each toe individually, calling them each a name in a language I'd never heard before: "Fumph, Kubaweiss, Applefoof . . ."

"Are you some kind of foot expert?"

"I studied a little shiatsu, you know . . . a little reflexology."

"So what's your grail?"

"Living and let living, rubbing a pretty girl's feet . . . you know. No, seriously though, I'm studying to be a beekeeper and I'm aiming to make the best honey in Canada."

I liked his patchouli flakiness and I was under the spell of his massage. This wasn't one of those foot-rub seduction routines either; I didn't feel like he was making any moves on me. Hippie love was exactly what I needed. Nurturing attention. Isobel might have been a bit bored, but I didn't care.

Jack and I slept out in the open that night. We unzipped our sleeping bags and zipped up one joint unibag, pretending it was necessary for warmth. The stars were out in full regalia: Orion, Little Dipper, Big Dipper, Cassiopeia. The fire crackled. In his arms, I felt the depression lifting, I had felt it lifting all night. I had the strange sensation that my forehead actually felt lighter, no longer shrouded. My eyes were heavy with a cozy sleep. I turned on my side, and Jack spooned me.

The next morning Isobel had the coffee going and the sandwich stuff out and ready. Jack was playing Hacky Sack by the lake. It was beautiful day. We decided to just drive a half-day and try to find another lake farther west to camp at.

I was ready to take the wheel, my lethargy had been replaced with effervescence. But Jack insisted; he said the pair of us had done a year's worth of driving in our almost cross-country tour.

As usual, nothing that interesting happened on the high-way. Cars mostly overtook us. Rosimund could never really get much beyond ninety-five klicks; plenty of people seemed like they wanted to drive like assholes at one hundred and ninety. We turtled along in Manitoba, back into the heart of the prairies. The hills were way behind us, and we knew we'd be flatlining for a long while now. Ahead was a mesmerizing heat haze on the asphalt. I realized it was actually nice to have so much space on the horizon, a person could really breathe and stretch out in this landscape.

The day went by slowly. Four hundred slow kilometres took us seven hours with pee stops and stretch breaks. It was pretty quiet mostly. I liked having Jack with us. He had nice energy. I liked the look of his arm on the stick shift. I liked his sun-kissed skin. He said he'd take us kayaking if we came out to visit him in Vancouver. Isobel said she'd need to find some waterproof lipstick first and a seal-tight container for smokes. Could we have cocktails on the river?

Around five o'clock, we parked in an isolated campsite on a small lakefront near Brandon. We wanted to have every lake experience we could before getting back to city life.

I was on fire duty and had managed to get a blaze going. Jack was collecting six suitably large rocks from the beach to heat in the fire for the hut as well as three metre-long sticks. Luckily we already had a plastic tarp.

We had a perfect hut location right on the sandy little nook in front of our site. Jack started off by digging a hole in the ground not too deep and fairly wide, then placed the three sticks in a circle surrounding the hole for the frame's structure, and then I covered them with the tarp so that it looked like a makeshift tent, which he sealed with logs. All that was left unsealed was the opening. Isobel meanwhile was chopping vegetables and garlic and wrapping parcels to be placed on the fire's grill. She made a parcel of brie and three salmon steak ones, which we'd splashed out on in town for our last night on the road.

While we waited for the food and the rocks to heat up enough, we got out our air mattress, blew it up, and threw it in the water. The sun was still intense, so we took turns floating around in the warm shallow water. If you waded far enough, you could almost manage to get submerged up to your belly button. After about ten good minutes of floating, I realized that my shoulders were for some reason tensed up to my ears, so I consciously lowered them, which then made me fall splashing in the water. Isobel had a good laugh that made her whole body wobble so much that she fell in too with a shriek. Jack played Hacky Sack on the sand. Iz and I frolicked and swam and had water fights until we exhausted ourselves and dinner was ready.

The food was awesome. I noticed that Isobel was breaking into her dinner with incredible oomph, like I'd never seen before. She even hogged most of the cheese. I was amazed. I didn't ask her why she was finally eating. I just watched the healthy glow of her puffed-out cheeks while she chewed and chewed. After dinner, we drank a little whisky to help digest.

The rocks were looking good and red—it was almost time

for hut. It was Isobel's first time, and she looked perturbed as I told her to take off all her clothes and climb underneath the blue tarp. Most first-time hutters found the experience a little frightening: the sudden heat, the opaque steam, scorching-hot air. Our three-man hut was fairly small, you had to crawl in and sit cross-legged and hunch-backed.

Jack and I carefully transported the rocks in a makeshift bucket/Frisbee from the firepit to the hole in the hut. I filled up a couple of empty Orangina bottles with water, took off my clothes, and crawled carefully into the hut. I had to admit, we had done a damn good job building the hut, though it was a little cramped. Funny thing about hut was that you didn't notice you were naked. I didn't think of it until I saw Isobel covering her breasts self-consciously. She was a skinny woman, beautiful but a bit surfboardlike with no roundy bits.

This was my first hut since the Sullivan days. I had missed it without realizing how much. I wanted her to love the hut experience as I did. I told her to breathe calmly, then I started gently pouring a stream of cool water on the burning rocks. The rocks hissed and let out a big cloud of super-hot steam. Instantly we were saturated in our own sweat. I had never been a sadistic hutter, like some who just keep pouring the water making the bouts of steam almost unbearably hot. I liked to pour a little at a time so you could enjoy each projection of steam and the after-effects of the lingering water in the air. I looked at Isobel through the fog and saw she looked confused.

"Don't worry about a thing, you'll learn to love hut," I reassured her. "It's great for the pores. Think of it like a spa!"

The steam was luxurious, I felt like I was swimming in it. I surrendered to it. I dripped and sweated and felt like I'd had a bucket of water poured over me and out of me. Jack was smiling beside me, sliding his wet hair back with his hand, his eyes closed. Isobel wasn't saying anything; she just looked at me wide-eyed.

After a while the rocks cooled, calming down; the water no longer sizzled much when it hit them. Wisps of steam lingered in the foggy hut, which we enjoyed until the last possible moment. You could understand how First Nations people used sweat lodges as sacred ritual places.

When the air was mostly clear, instead of crawling out of the hut, Jack decided to break out of it. On the count of three we pulled the tarp free from the logs and were blasted with one of those amazing prairie sunsets of peachy, saffrony, orangey hues spanning the whole sky above.

We were wowed by the brightness and beauty of it. We whooped cement-cracking screams as we charged into the water. This was one of the best post-hut experiences I've ever had, in my all-time top five. Having sweated every possible toxin out of my body, I felt totally invigorated. The coldness of the water crashed with our body heat. This was living. Isobel and I even peed standing up, side by side. Jack frolicked in the surf.

Isobel went to eat what was left of the food, and Jack and I played naked Hacky Sack on the beach. I was having a ridiculously good time. I wanted to play naked Frisbee next. The vibe had subtly changed: sex was in the air. I felt desire rev me up. I didn't feel at all self-conscious with him. It was weird. I knew I didn't have a magazine body. My legs weren't very long. Even with Mount Vesuvius reddening the left side of my face, I loved myself.

After Hacky-Sacking, we jumped back in the lake to clean off the sweat. It was colder now. I worried a bit about bloodsuckers. I could see that Isobel had gone to bed inside the tent. We came back and sat in front of the fire. Jack took my hand and caressed it. He was sitting on a log.

"You're gorgeous, girl. I don't know what you're thinking, but I'd . . ."

"Me too. Let's have another drink." I grabbed the whisky and chugged some down. Jack had a big gulp too.

I straddled him.

He kissed my neck hungrily. I could've cried, it felt so good. He kept at it for ages until I was pretty wound up. His other hand stroked my hair. Our chests pressed together were warm. My wet hair dripped down my back, but the fire's flames and our skin on skin were heating me.

I wasn't going to fall in love with this guy. This was just for the wonderful moment. He moaned when I reached down and cupped his balls. "That's some fine Hacky action you got down there, we could . . ."

"Oh, Annie. Wow. Can I just?"

"I'd like that a lot . . ."

He grabbed a condom out of his knapsack, ripped it open with his teeth, rolled it on, and then slipped inside me. I rocked back and forth, feeling us as one fluid rhythm. With my face buried in his hair that smelled wonderfully like damp cedar, we moved like that for a sweet while until the fever picked up. He grabbed my ass and bit down lightly on my right nipple, not too hard, not too soft. I started coming and coming and freefalling off a cliff. Inside I yelled, HALLELUJAH!!!

His grasp tightened as his orgasm thundered in just behind mine. He shook. He shook some more. He let out a gleeful "Yeeeeeeseeeeeeeeeeeeeeeeeee!!!" as we rolled off the tree stump into the sand behind.

When we were done panting, I grabbed his hand and hoisted him up to go for a final skinny dip. Then we lay in each other's arms in our unibag and slept peacefully.

We dropped off Jack in a small Saskatchewan town where he was visiting a pal of his (he was couch-surfing for the summer). He gave us some sagebrush from inside his backpack to hang from the rear-view mirror, telling us to throw away those chemical air fresheners. I waved goodbye and revelled in flash-backs of the night before. He had done me good, and I felt well and truly detoxed.

Later that day we stopped at a hardware store to get supplies for the car, some duct tape for the left wing mirror and some Krazy Glue for the gear stick top thingy that had popped off. We found a ToolMart in a strip mall called Damascus. I walked in and almost immediately felt uncomfortable. Fluorescent lighting. Endless aisles of useless stuff. How would we ever find anything? It was dizzying. Isobel hunted for a helper person, but it seemed like they were all on a break. There was one guy with a headset on and a queue of five agro-looking tool shoppers. So we combed the aisles. I wanted to get out of there quickly. I wanted to find our tools and get the hell out. They were playing something almost recognizable on the overhead speakers.

The old familiar dizzy feeling was coming for me. Isobel stalked off like a flamingo, in a new walk she was working on. She was going to find the duct tape, and I was in charge of looking for Krazy Glue.

This one came out of nowhere.

The usual shit happened:

My heart pounded. My neck sweated.

My hearing amplified.

The loudspeakers were playing the Cowboy Junkies.

I fell to the ground, almost on purpose.

Is this it?

Is this me, mad? Am I foaming? Are they going to take me away to the loony bin?

I finally just gave up.

I huddled into fetal.

There was nobody in my aisle. The floor was lino, fake wood colour. I think it must have been cleaned that morning; it smelt lemony in a hideously antiseptic way. I was oddly alert, watching all of my movements. My mind had separated from my body. I couldn't order it to do anything, it just wanted to lie still in the fetal position.

I was in a zone. Time had stopped. I knew I was prostrate on the floor of a ToolMart. There were bound to be ramifications.

The fluorescent light pulsed in time with my boil. The product names orbed around me. UFIXIT, SQUEAK-NO-MORE, SMALL HEAD, DIBBITS . . . They fed into a river of my worst fears.

I was insane.

I was too embarrassed to shout for help. Time was going by though. I was less sure I wanted to be found. I was surprised I could be lying on the ground in a public place and nobody would notice. When would Isobel come get me? Would the store staff find me first?

I was having a nervous breakdown. Wasn't someone going to notice?

What is a nervous breakdown anyway? For a moment I forgot myself and listened to the Cowboy Junkies's wonderfully husky "Sweet Jane."

My memory rewound to lying on my back as a small child, being dragged around the neighbourhood on a sled looking up at the sundogs, bewildered by the crystallized snow flakes, prisms falling from the sky. I was wearing a full body ski suit, rainbow-coloured. I had warm mittens that my mom had attached to a string and sewn into my sleeves so I wouldn't ever lose them. I wore four pairs of socks and sheepskin wool boots. I had on full-body long johns and a turtleneck. The only part of me that was exposed were my two cheeks. My nostril hairs felt crunchy from the freezing weather. The sky was blue. The sound of the plastic sled squeaking along the pavements over smooth, hardened snow. The feeling of bumps underneath my back. Mom was taking me to the IGA for fun and groceries. I loved being carted around on my back seeing underneath people's cars. Dogs looked huge and I liked to look at trees' feet.

Then when I grew up and met Sullivan, I told him about my happy sled memories. Our first winter together he showed up outside my apartment with a big wooden sled and he took me to the park. It was nine o'clock and all the lessons and hockey matches were long over. We had the rink to ourselves. He put on his skates, took a massive candle out of his backpack, and skated to the middle of the lake and put it there and lit it. He had a mini-boombox too. He put on "Sweet Jane" and skated back to me. I lay flat on the sled that fit me perfectly. It was a mild night, probably around minus ten. Cold but not fuckfuckfuckfuck cold. Before we'd gone out he made me put on two pairs of long johns and two pairs of socks. We had toques and gloves, we were well geared up. He had a rope attached to the sled that he tied around his waist. He skated around and around the rink and that big candle. I stared at the stars, listened to his breathing.

"Are you sure I'm not too heavy?"

"Light as a feather. This is good training for hockey season."

Afterwards we sat together and drank cocoa from his flask until our asses were so cold we were worried about getting hemorrhoids. We went home and shared a hot bath.

This was all wrong. I was a twenty-four-year-old woman, taken down by panic attacks. It wasn't like my life sucked. I had loved ones. I had legs, arms, a brain.

Anger joined my fear.

I ordered myself to sit up.

I sat up.

It was that simple.

I could almost conjure what this dragon of smoke and fear looked like, like a heat haze on the horizon in a blobby translucent shape. It wasn't even a real hallucination, I knew that, but I needed to conjure something tangible for me to scream as loud as possible at in my head: Give me your best shot, you goddamned FUCKING BULLY. You're all smoke, you got NOTHING. What's the worst thing you can do to me?

DO YOU HEAR ME? FUUUUUUUUUUUUUUUCKKKKK YOUUUUUU! To my surprise I felt the dragon retreating, melting into a puddle of silent nothingness.

The adrenalin had mellowed, and I felt an endorphin surge, like you do after running. I saw some packages of Krazy Glue on the shelf right in front of me. I grabbed one and stood up.

It was easy. I was a Phoenix rising.

I smiled at the ToolMart staff guy who was walking up the aisle to check on me. His nametag said his name was Paul.

"Can I help you with anything, miss?"

"No, I just found what I needed."

"Are you sure you're all right?"

I looked up at the ceiling to see if they had surveillance cameras. They did. I was on film being a wacko.

"I just have low blood pressure. Sometimes my heart forgets to pump at all, and then I get a little flimsy. What's it like working here?"

"Not bad, you know, I get overtime and stuff. I'd rather be skateboarding, but a guy's gotta make the rent, y'know."

"Ya, I hear you."

"Do you want some water or anything?"

"Nah, I'm good, I'm gonna go hook up with my friend."

Isobel was busy at the till paying the cashier for the duct tape.

"I just need to pop through the mall to grab some music," I told her.

"Now?"

"Yup."

I went to the record store and found a copy of *Moondance*. Reclaiming was my new agenda. Reclaiming sex, hut, and music from the Sullivan–Annie grip.

We drove through the rest of the province in silence. Hot air blasted through the windows, but I felt a hint of autumn in the air. The colours at their full peak. Overripe and bursting with green and yellow. The fields waiting for harvest. Weeds shoulder-high. I scratched my mosquito bites and listened to the tape back to back to back to back—three hundred and fifty kilometres worth (which felt like fifty-seven times, give or take). Isobel didn't ask what it was all about. She respected my music mission.

By the third time through, I didn't think of Sullivan. Aversion therapy was working. Plus I had gone head to head with the panic dragon and I had kicked ass. I knew I'd carved new ground that day in ToolMart.

I drove on, with Isobel at my side eating white cheddar popcorn meditatively. "You know, I could be deluding myself, but I think I'm kind of missing Finn. Il me manque." Those wondrously green eyes of hers glistened. Was it fatigue or emotion? I wondered.

"That's gotta be a new experience for you, I've never heard you express that kind of sentiment before."

"I'm not sure what's with me, I'm eating like a maniac, I'm thinking nostalgic thoughts about Finn. Maybe I'm coming down with something."

"Whatever you do, you can't mess with that boy's head anymore. He's our friend now. Buddies are sacred. Plus they're might be a professional element to our relationship now . . . I've had some thoughts . . ."

"What are you talking about?"

I didn't answer. I wanted to ponder more before I spilled.

We drove on in comfortable silence past towns and fields and endless highway and prairie. Old red and grey barns dotted the landscape. Grain silos and cows. The road went on and on. We drove and drove. The air cooled, the light changed. At our next pee stop by the side of the highway, something ran right past my foot as I squatted between the open door and the car. A lizard with black stripes. Was it my lucky prairie skink after all?!

Crossing back over into rat-free Alberta, we were ready to get home. The road was deforming my back. The vinyl upholstery was burning my skin. I was out of the funk, ready to get going on something, a project, a grail, something not romance-focused. Meanwhile, I romanticized my new take on life. Imagined myself as endlessly fulfilled, feisty like Ani DiFranco. An independent heroine, with no need ever for a boyfriend. Of course, in my scenario, countless men tried to woo me, but to no avail. Until the One. It was going to take some effort to recondition my fantasy life.

Restless energy in a car was no good. I needed to be out walking the streets, panic-free. Living, making the most of my life. I was going to be disciplined, only watch a maximum of three videos a week. And sit-ups, I would do five hundred a day. I was going to build up my core strength. And sun salutations too, ten every hour.

As Isobel drove past the small towns leading us back to our northern town, I had the urge to write something down, to put it all to rest. I brainstormed drivel for miles. How did they do it, songwriters?

> You were a great lover
> To not just me
> But I love you
> See you, so long
> I left you in a field somewhere in the middle
> Of Al-berrrrrrrrrrr-ta
> See you, so long
> Time to keep on truckin'

I groaned. I had no sense of poetry, no musicality. For all my music-lyric education, I was goddamned hopeless. Maybe Finn could help. It could be a genre problem. I needed to choose between an angry punk song or something sweet and commemorative. I picked up Finn's guitar and for the first time tried to play something. My fingers didn't want to contort properly. I soon gave up. I needed serious training.

"Let's go straight to Finn's," I said.

On the last leg to E-town, I lay back and made plans, plans for our reform. Discipline, hard work, less movie-watching, and lots of training. Surely enthusiasm could override lack of talent. Isobel had the obvious makings of a diva: she'd been sustaining her own fan club since she was a teenager.

The Cadillac Couches. It was the name I had secretly always thought would be perfect for a band. Everyone spends all this time with their butts happily planted on their sumptuous couches dreaming their dreams. Couches can be vehicles for transcendental visions. Mostly though, in reality, dreamers drive trusty bangers, not Cadillacs.

I thought Finn would like it too. We could go on tour and one day open for Ani. We could get a Boogie van. We would cross the country all the way to the Maritimes and back. I could break guitar strings, I could restring my guitar. I could cover my fingers in duct tape and look really tough. I could tune my guitar and tell jokes. I could rock out for real, instead of just air-guitaring. We'd have groupies, party with other musicians, write meaningful songs. We would get to Florence at last and busk! We could . . .

Maybe we'd never get out of the basement or the garage, but dreaming is free like we rock chicks like to say.

"Now, Isobel, I've got something serious to discuss with you. Picture this: you in a houndstooth mini-skirt, go-go boots, a leather bustier, and a plum-coloured boa, standing at the microphone . . ."

Isobel's eyes twinkled as I filled her head with a vision of chick-rock-stardom and Edwardian corsetry with a post-modern twist.

Home
8,207 kms total!

We pulled into town at 4:00 AM, too late and too tired to go to Finn's. I dropped off Isobel at her place and drove the few blocks to mine. I walked in to a quiet house; my roommates were asleep or out. I dragged myself into my bedroom and fell on the bed. There was something crinkly beneath my head. A pile of official-looking letters from the credit card companies and a mysterious purple envelope. Of course, Hawksley's letter!

I turned on the light. I allowed myself a little surge of excitement, one last throwback to my former mission.

It was a form letter on Hawksley Workman official stationary.

Thank you for your missive,
dear fellow Love Adventurer.
May you travel well on your magic carpet.
May the music be your soundtrack with the angels.
XOXO H

I read it a few times. In the past I might have smelled it, or tried to eat it even, but my turtle shell had finally hardened. I was an evolved young woman, no longer an hysterical tragedian. Panic had lost its hold on me. I was going to face life again, in a new incarnation: intergalactic rock star.

"ooo wah ooo"

The Cadillac Couches

Afterword
One Year Later

Tilt *Magazine* Vol. 25, Autumn
Shell Shocked by Ama-Rock on Stage 9
Edmonton Folk Festival
Review by Ursula V
Rating: ???*!

This year's annual Edmonton Folk Festival showcased some sounds never heard before. Stage 9's two o'clock Sunday slot was filled by interloping balladeers who call themselves The Cadillac Couches, their gospel—a celebration of cacophony.

The sweaty sweet smell of ganja emanated from a small, unsuspecting crowd sprawled out on tarps, talking, cloud-sculpting, and waiting for the next band to hit Stage 9. Traditionally a stage for the lesser known artists, people gravitate to Stage 9 for that reason, to hear the next big thing.

Ten minutes late The Cadillac Couches *stumbled* on to the stage. Guitarist Annie Jones wore a forest green T-shirt with the slogan *Anyone Can Make Art* in block letters printed across her chest. Her skin colour almost matched her T-shirt; she had the look of someone who was deeply seasick. Wearing a zebra-strapped Gibson, she headed for stage left, as near the edge as possible—like she was plotting her escape route through the river valley. The lead singer and front woman, Isobella Sparks, strutted up to centrestage wearing a fuchsia-coloured boa over a leather bustier and pink hot pants. She sported '50s cat-eye sunglasses and black Puss-in-Boots stilettos. With a permanent pout and her jet-black Cleopatra hairdo, she was a study in rock sirendom. A drummer completed this oddball trio. Wearing a black vinyl suit with a tomato in his lapel, Finn Hingley obscured himself behind an over-the-top drum kit that looked like a futuristic Lego space station with a galaxy of noise-making percussive components.

Jones started off their first song by tapping her foot on a wa-wa pedal, making a '70s-style funky intro. Away they blasted with "Tumbleweeds," one of their two original numbers. The rest of their set list was made up of barely recognizable cover versions of love angst songs. They massacred their way through Patsy Cline's "Crazy," blasphemingly tortured the crowd with Nina Simone's "To Love Somebody," and peaked in badness, butchering The Police's "Every Breath You Take" by fusing it with Roberta Flack's "The First Time." They managed to shred Van Morrison's "Someone Like You" both times they played it. It was almost as appallingly bad as their version of "Wild Is the Wind."

The Cadillac Couches jumbled lyrics, fused melodies, harmonized inappropriately, had no chordal riffs, did too many acrobatic leaps, high-fived way too much, and seemed wholly unapologetic. Initially, the crowd couldn't believe what they were being subjected to. Some of the more rabid people spoke out:

"HEY—LEARN some chords!" heckled a guy wearing a Calgary Flames hockey shirt.

"Why don't you take some MUSIC LESSONS! You guys suuuuck!" yelled a disgruntled muso.

"Gee whiz. C'mon, guys they're just learning," cried a middle-aged, good-citizen family man wearing a Tilley hat.

The heckling petered out as half the audience left. The tide turned and the remaining audience got on the Couches' wavelength, feeling the strange noises in their hips and groins. They threw themselves into the anarchy, participating by screaming in nonsensical call and response. A lone pair of stripy boxer shorts hit the stage and triggered an infectious general underwear evacuation, during which Hingley managed to do a rain-stick solo for over three minutes. It was a moment topped by Sparks, who in a misguided flash tried to wrap her lips around a didgeridoo, mock fellating it. She emoted pure dominatrix—whenever she shimmied near the drummer, he percussed himself in the head.

Jones, clearly exhilarated, did a series of Pete Townsend leaps in the air. The Cadillac Couches couldn't have looked any happier. Their frenzy was infectious— the crowd pogoed deliriously.

One fan jumped on stage right and did a series of perfect cartwheels before exiting stage left, uninjured. The crowed roared. A thin guy with a pencil moustache and lime green pants hoisted himself on stage and stood there ready to do something, but tragically lost his nerve, ran to the other side of the stage and jumped off, running into the distance.

After a modest fifteen-song atonal set with six repeats, The Cadillac Couches clasped hands and together yelled: "THANK YOU, EDMONTON!" Unbelievably, the crowd wanted more and insisted on encores! So they did it all over again: Patsy, Elvis . . .

The festival program blurb explained who these musical anarchists were. All this brouhaha was a deliberate effort by the Edmonton Folk Festival organizers to be non-elitist. As part of a new initiative, the organizers introduced a new music workshop: the Amateur Stage, to find new talent and to host a live karaoke band. The organizers chose The Cadillac Couches to host the jam because of their obvious musical hopelessness as well as an eloquent letter written by Finn Hingley telling of their universal plight: infinite enthusiasm, no talent. Hingley argued that people were tired of being spectators to the spectacle, they wanted to join in, to get off their asses and in front of a mike.

When asked what she thought about the necessity in art for quality control, Sparks said, "It's completely naive to think like that. Our oeuvre is more performance art. Think DADA."

Eventually, The Cadillac Couches took their bow— beaming at the grass on the way down and the big Alberta sky all the way back up.

After Afterword
Many Years Later

DJ Annie's shambolic soundtrack mix for *Cadillac Couches*: a starter selection of past and future tunes in random order for music freaks . . .

"Just the Other Day" | Jr. Gone Wild
"Where's Me Jumper" | Sultans of Ping
"Ooh Wah Baby," "Roll with the Punches" | Ben Sures
"Alberta" | Eric Clapton
"Diamond Smiles" | Boomtown Rats
"Crash Into Me" | Dave Matthews Band
"Thorn in My Side" | Eurythmics
"Trumpets" | The Waterboys
"Nobody's Baby," "Into My Arms" | Nick Cave
"Lights of Montreal" | Luann Kowalek
"Andy," "C'est Comme Ça" | Les Rita Mitsouko
"Bye Bye Mon Cowboy" | Mitsou
"Tiger Woods," "Jerusalem," "I'm Not the Guy," "Talkin'
    Woody, Bob, Bruce & Dan Blues" | Dan Bern
"Now and Forever," "Cynthia," "Diamond Mind" | Blue Rodeo
"Tight Knit Seams" | Old Reliable
"Don't Be Crushed," "Paper Shoes," "No Sissies," "Safe and
    Sound" | Hawksley Workman
"Both Hands," "Buildings and Bridges," "Out of Range," "Not
    a Pretty Girl" | Ani DiFranco
The Ghost of Tom Joad (whole album) | Bruce Springsteen
"Should I Stay or Should I Go," "I Fought the Law" | The Clash
"Queer" | Rheostatics

"Handle with Care" | Jenny Lewis with The Watson Twins
"Jesus," "Beauty," "Fromage" | Hookahman
"Cold Cold Ground," "Jersey Girl," "Downtown Train"
    | Tom Waits
"Hey Good Lookin'" | Hank Williams
"Left and Leaving," "Watermark" | The Weakerthans
"You Look Like Rain" | Morphine
"Lilac Wine" | Jeff Buckley
"Churchill" | Greg Macpherson
"Lay Lady Lay," "Tangled Up in Blue" | Bob Dylan
"Shopping Trolley" | Beth Orton
"Mailbox" | Paul Bellows
"That Time" | Regina Spektor
"Bloody Motherfucking Asshole" | Martha Wainwright
"A Boy Named Sue" | Johnny Cash
"Jackson" | Johnny Cash and June Carter Cash
"To Love Somebody," "Ain't Got No/I Got Life" | Nina Simone
"Mandinka" | Sinead O'Connor
"Ne Me Quittes Pas" | Jacques Brel
"Into the Mystic" | Van Morrison
"Easy Skanking" | Bob Marley
"Don't Go," "Movies" | Hothouse Flowers
"Indoor Fireworks," "I Want You," "Blue Chair," "Everyday I
    Write the Book" | Elvis Costello
"Your Revolution" | DJ Vadim
"Satellite" | Danny Michele
"The Eye in Magpie" | Electricity for Everybody
"Teenage Kicks" | The Undertones
"Distillation" | Erin McKeown
"The Man Who Sold the World" | Nirvana

"Right on Time," "Car Wheels on a Gravel Road"
  | Lucinda Williams
"Mundian to Bach Ke" | Panjabi MC
"My Drug Buddy" | The Lemonheads
"Unknown Legend" | Neil Young
"Better Man" | Pearl Jam
"Tomber la Chemise" | Zebda
"Wear Clean Draws" | The Coup
"Reuben" | Cathy Davey
"Trouble" | Ray LaMontagne
"Wild Is the Wind" | David Bowie
"The First Time" | Roberta Flack
"Isabelle," "Think About You" | Jean LeLoup
"Fight for Your Right" | Beastie Boys
"As Tears Roll By" | Daniel Lanois
"One" | U2
"A Good Heart" | Feargal Sharkey
"Killing Floor," "Built for Comfort" | Howlin' Wolf
"Damn Sam," "Come Pick Me Up" | Ryan Adams
"Hey, That's No Way to Say Goodbye" | Leonard Cohen
(Some of these songs are cover versions.)

DJ Annie doesn't know when to stop so will leave it here, with
  this song:
"Thank You For Your Love" | Antony and the Johnsons

Song Credits

The author wishes to thank these artists for permission to quote excerpts from their songs: "Jerusalem" from *Dan Bern*, © Dan Bern, 1997; "Don't be Crushed" from *For Him and the Girls*, © Hawksley Workman, 2000; "True Revolutionaries" from *Smartie Mine*, © Dan Bern, 1998; "Talkin' Alien Abduction Blues" from *Dog Boy Van*, © Dan Bern, 1997; "Ooh Wah Baby" from *Ooh Wah Baby*, © Ben Sures, 1998; "Both Hands" from *Ani DiFranco*, © Ani DiFranco, 1990; "Providence" from *Providence*, © Luann Kowalek, 1994; "You Had Time" from *Out of Range*, © Ani DiFranco, 1994; "Paper Shoes" from *For Him and the Girls*, © Hawksley Workman, 2000; "If He Tries Anything" from *Out of Range*, © Ani DiFranco, 1994; "Not a Pretty Girl" from *Not a Pretty Girl* © Ani DiFranco, 1995; "Blood in the Boardroom" from *Puddle Dive* © Ani DiFranco, 1993; "Untouchable Face" from *Dilate*, © Ani DiFranco, 1996; "Aside" from *Left and Leaving*, © The Weakerthans, 2000.

"She'll Be Coming 'Round the Mountain" derives from an old African-American spiritual and nineteenth-century American folk song.

The author wishes to thank and recognize the Provost and Scholars of King's College, Cambridge, and the Society of Authors as the Literary Representative of the Estate of E.M. Forster for the permission to quote *A Room with a View*, 1908, and *Howards End*, 1910.

The author also wishes to acknowledge that her characters misquote/paraphrase dialogue from *Bullets Over Broadway*, Woody Allen and Douglas McGrath © 1994, and from *Withnail and I*, Bruce Robinson © 1987.

The references from Emily Dickinson and John Keats fall in the public domain.

Acknowledgments

I am bursting with gratitude to the universe. And to loads of people.

Thank you, Ruth Linka, for being a dream-maker and holding down the Canada fort for me and for being such an amazing beacon of hard, noble work. Thank you, Pete Kohut, for the gorgeous cover and Emily Shorthouse, Cailey Cavallin, and all of the Brindle & Glass publishing team for your hard work.

Huge thanks to Lynne Van Luven for her expert editing and sculpting guidance! Big thanks to Heather Sangster for the wonderfully attentive copyediting and proofing.

Thank you to the Alberta Foundation for the Arts, Edmonton Arts Council, Edmonton Artist Trust Fund, and Banff Centre for the Arts Writing Program for their support and encouragement. Jane Bisbee, Vern Thiessen, and Paul Pearson, wonderful helpers for the arts.

Thank you to Duncan Turner and my former colleagues at the BPAA for all the support and wisdom, I miss you guys! Kathy Shute would win hands down the best boss/mentor worldwide award if there were one.

Thank you, Mom and Dad and brother Martin, for the love and all that Watson-ness and for surrounding me with books books books. And big thanks to Dad for the best gift ever, the babysitting fund that buys me time to myself to write. Huge thanks to our own Mary Poppins Blanaid Hennessy!

For all the super love and support, thank you, Irish family–Youghalees and Dubliners alike.

Huge thanks and big love to bff J-girl. Thanks for speaking the same language and being there always.

And thanks to MW for all that early inspiration.

Thank you, beloved Parisians, English pals, E-town buddies for life, BC sisters, and friends all around the world for all the love.

Thank you, Sheffieldians and Rob Watson, for putting me on a cosmic trail to find creative fulfillment and the best husband ever.

Thank you, ES, for your confidence-engendering love and guidance.

Thank you, stepsisters, for being so inspiring in so many ways.

Thank you, Andrew Struthers, for being so damn smart and such a good teacher.

Thank you, U of A English department, especially Kristjana Gunnars and Ted Bishop.

RK, you and your Bath Spa team were better than I could have conjured. CD, you rocked my writing world with your generous and insightful feedback. Bath Spa Spring Chickens, thanks for those helpful and fun-filled jamming sessions.

Thank you, JK, for showing me how to choose the creative path, and for the big bad love too.

Lorne and Vanessa, you are not gone, you are always with me, especially when listening to music, which is most of the time.

Thanks to everyone I have forgotten to mention.

Thank you to all the musicians whose lyrics I quote and to Ben S. for all his encyclopedic help and affection. Also, infinite thanks to all the amazing musicians/directors/writers who feed my soul every day.

Thank you, Aengus, for choosing me and for being who you are, an amazing man, awesome husband, my own personal editor extraordinaire, and love of my life. And thank you, Toto and Felix, you gorgeous little monkeys are my giant joy-makers.

SOPHIE B. WATSON is an award-winning freelance writer who has been published in several magazines, including *briarpatch*, *Canadian Dimension*, *Canadian Living*, *Legacy Magazine*, and *The Sustainable Times* (among others). She holds a degree in English and French literature from the University of Alberta as well as a master's in creative writing from Bath Spa University. She has been a library page, a waitress, a substitute DJ, a bookseller, and, most recently, the editor of Cork University Press. *Cadillac Couches* is Sophie's first novel. Read more about Sophie (and her aquatic larks) on her blog at sophiebwatson.com.